WELCOMED AT GUNPOINT

Suddenly a great commotion of cawing birds shattered Kit's thoughts as once again a cloud of black feathers spiraled for the sky. Instantly Kit wheeled around, bringing his rifle to bear...and froze where he stood.

Kit had been so intent on what he was doing that he had been completely unaware of the fifteen armed warriors who had been easing their way toward him. It was only when the crows scattered that he had had any notion of them at all, and by then it was too late. There was no chance to run, and fighting was hopeless since every one of the warriors carried a musket. But they were Flathead Indians, and the Flatheads were one of the few tribes that had accepted the white trappers and even welcomed them onto their lands.

These particular Flathead warriors, however, did not have that "welcoming" look on their scowling faces. It was more a look of murder!

Book 3

Doug Hawkins = Douglas Hirt
(pen name)

KIT CARSON

REDCOAT RENEGADES
DOUG HAWKINS

LEISURE BOOKS

NEW YORK CITY

*For Beth Anne and
Colleen*

A LEISURE BOOK®

March 1998

Published by

Dorchester Publishing Co., Inc.
276 Fifth Avenue
New York, NY 10001

ISBN 0-8439-4368-8

The name "Leisure Books" and the stylized "L" with design are
trademarks of Dorchester Publishing Co., Inc.

Printed in the United States of America.

ACKNOWLEDGMENTS

My sincerest thanks to the late Dr. Thomas Edward, who so graciously allowed me to roam freely through his rare and valuable collection of monographs by that nineteenth-century Native American scholar, professor W. G. F. Smith.

KIT CARSON

REDCOAT RENEGADES

Chapter One

At one time his friends jokingly referred to him as "the pirate."

Alexander Smythe *did* look the part of a swaggering cutthroat, prowling the pitching deck of a merchant marauder along the Spanish Main; a rogue who owed loyalty to no man, no country, and to whom the Jolly Roger was the only ensign of allegiance.

But Smythe was not widely known by that name these days, since he had lost most of his old friends and he never bothered to make any new ones.

And the reason he had no close friends was that over the years Smythe *had* became too much like his nickname.

Smythe stood six feet, one inch, a fifty-year-old mountain man whose barrel-chested breadth was slowly gravitating south toward his wide, black belt, where a pistol, a Sheffield butcher knife, and a bat-

tered, shortened Wilkerson saber now resided. He had
left the foremost six inches of the blade embedded in
a Yankee's spine where he had broken it off more
than twenty years before. Rather than discarding the
sword, Smythe had merely ground a new point onto
it. He preferred the weapon shorter anyway.

Smythe had come to this land in 1811, fought the
Americans in 1812, lost an eye and left the lower half
of his right leg lying on the battlefield at Frenchtown
in 1813. Today, a graying red beard encircled his
face, a stained black patch crudely hid the empty eye
socket, and a peg whittled from an oak tree and fastened comfortably below his knee served sufficiently
well for Smythe's purposes. And if it were not for the
buckskins that Smythe clad himself in these days, and
the tall sorrel horse instead of a tall ship upon which
he rode, the visage of a pirate would have been complete.

But then, who says pirates only sailed the high
seas?

"Wot's the matter, Gov'nor?" Aston Marsten inquired when Smythe suddenly reined to a halt and
cocked an ear toward the stand of dark trees along
the trail they had been following. Smythe squinted in
concentration, his single eye nearly shutting as he
strained to catch some distant sound. Behind him the
line of mounted trappers—eight in number, not count-
ing the pack animals—pulled their horses to a stop.

Marsten was a sharp-featured man who appeared
as if he was always staring into a bright light. On
those rare occasions that he did fully open his eyes,
one would have been surprised to discover that they
were really a dark blue instead of black, as they most
often appeared. He'd spent his youth in Liverpool un-

til the night he'd murdered a seafaring man in a pub on the waterfront over a pint of ale accidentally spilled onto his brogans. One jump ahead of the constables, Marsten had stowed away on a ship bound for Vancouver, and upon arriving in the wilderness of North America, he'd taken a job with the Hudson's Bay Company.

But that was all ancient history now. Like most men with the Company, Marsten had adapted well, becoming more Indian than white in his eighteen years this side of the pond. That other life—the one he had fled from back in England—was no more than a fuzzy memory now.

"You hear that?" Smythe asked softly.

"Wot? I don't hear nothin'."

"Dismount." Smythe swung off his horse. As the other men gathered around, he pointed to Marsten and a third man, a young Canadian named Wilber Port. "You two come with me. The rest of you stay here." Taking his heavy buffalo rifle with him, Smythe started into the forest, moving silently in the peculiar rowing gait he'd adopted after losing the leg, his peg leaving neat, round tracks in the hard earth.

They traveled several hundred yards in silence, Smythe musing that the very day that Yankee shrapnel had plucked out half his sight, he'd been given twice the hearing. And there must have been some truth to that, for Smythe had ears keener than any other man he knew. Suddenly he stopped and dropped to his haunches, the two other men joining him.

"Wot's you onto?"

"Listen."

At first Marsten and Port heard only the muffled

sounds of the forest around them, then Port, having the younger ears, all at once lifted his eyebrows in surprise and said softly, "Voices. I hear them now. Sounds like Injuns."

"Got to be Flatheads," Marsten observed. "They're the only ones in this neck o' the woods."

Smythe motioned them along. The voices grew louder, and soon the words became clear.

"Flatheads, all right," Marsten whispered as they bellied up to the top of a ridge and looked down at the two men busily dressing out a buck deer they had recently brought down. An arrow still protruded from its brown hide. Nearby, their horses were cropping the short grass.

"These two are from Calling Elk's band," Smythe noted. "I've see that one before." His thick English accent was in direct conflict with his rough dress of buckskin and wool.

Port let go a sigh of relief and whispered, "At least they ain't hostile. Reckon we ought to be getting back to the others?" he asked, glancing at the one-eyed captain of the fur brigade.

But Smythe had other thoughts.

Below, the two braves had set aside their weapons: bows and arrows, and a "London Fusil" that still looked brand new. It was one of the many such guns provided to Calling Elk's people by the Hudson's Bay Company; a dozen beaver pelts bought one gun. But lately Smythe had been lowering the price for Calling Elk's band, and now almost every brave owned at least one of the Company's trade guns.

Smythe's single gray eye narrow at Port. "It would be unneighborly not to go down there and have a powwow with our Flathead friends, now wouldn't it?'' His lips compressed into a hard, thin line that hitched up on one corner.

Port swallowed hard at the treachery that clearly laced Smythe's words.

Marsten grinned savagely. "I'd say it would be downright unconscionable not to go down there and smoke a peace pipe with them blokes, Gov'nor.''

The three trappers started down. Below, the two Flathead warriors glanced up, startled by the sight of them. They reached for their weapons, then, upon recognizing Smythe, relaxed some and stood, waiting.

"Smythe, it is you,'' one of the braves said when the trio drew up.

"Looks like you've had some good hunting,'' Smythe said, studying the half-butchered deer. "You're with Calling Elk's band, ain't you? I don't believe I remember your name.''

"I'm called Many Arrows.''

"And I am Swift Water Running,'' the other announced.

"I know you,'' Port said to this second Indian. "We passed a bottle of whiskey with some of your friends in your camp last winter.''

Swift Water Running grinned and nodded his head, recalling the incident. "You have whiskey now?'' he asked eagerly.

Marsten frowned. "Naw, don't hardly ever see much of that, except wot we can steal from the Company's storerooms. Doc McLoughlin only allows us two pints a year, and that's gone down into our bellies the first day we get back to Fort Vancouver.'' He gave Smythe a sly look. "You don't got any whiskey for these friends of ours, do you?''

Smythe leaned upon his long rifle, considering. He

13

rocked back on the peg leg, then screwed up his mouth behind the red and gray whiskers. With an unholy glint in his gray eye which he slanted briefly toward Marsten, he said, "I've a bottle back with my gear, boys. Come along with us and get yourself a drink."

The deer immediately forgotten, the two Indians grabbed up their bows and the fusil and anxiously started back with Smythe. Port stepped off a few feet to the left and moved ahead, as if trying to distance himself from the party. Marsten dropped behind, unnoticed while Smythe held their attention with some idle chatter. Soon the waiting trappers and horses appeared through the thinning trees.

Smythe halted his odd, rowing gait. "You wait here, boys. I don't want the others to know that I'm bringing you two a bottle." Smythe hesitated, casting a glance around at Port and Marsten. The sudden uneasiness that settled over them was so heavy, even the two Flatheads felt it. Many Arrows gripped the fusil tighter, his wary eyes taking in the position of the three white men. Swift Water Running sensed something was up, too, and slowly reached for an arrow from the quiver across his shoulder.

"Now!" Smythe ordered.

Behind Swift Water Running, Marsten's rifle boomed. Swift Water Running lurched forward as a fist-size hole ripped apart his breast.

Many Arrows wheeled, momentarily riveted by the sight of his partner lurching forward; shocked by this unprovoked attack by supposedly friendly trappers. But his shock lasted only a split second before a savage sense of revenge took its place. He instantly drew back the hammer of his flintlock.

"Port!" Smythe snapped when the other trapper hesitated. In another second it would be too late. The Indian's musket was already coming up toward Smythe. In a flash, the peg-legged trapper yanked the glistening saber from its sheath and, moving faster than most men his size could, pivoted upon the oaken stake below his knee and lashed out, knocking the barrel up at the same time its deafening explosion engulfed him in a cloud of smoke and a hot ball seared his cheek. Pivoting again, Smythe swung the honed edge of steel at the Indian's neck. Flesh parted beneath its force and only Many Arrows's vertebrae stopped the blade from passing completely through.

Many Arrows collapsed into a crumpled pile like a puppet with its strings cut, his still-beating heart sending a crimson fountain into the air, striving mightily to drain his body of every last drop of blood.

Port came over. Smythe wheeled and struck out, hitting the man between the eyes with the hilt of his saber.

"The next time that happens," he growled, bending over the fallen trapper and resting the point of his saber upon his chest, "I'll have your bloody heart, and that's a promise, Mr. Port!"

By this time the other trappers had swarmed around them. They wheeled to a stop, staring at the two dead Indians.

"What happened here, Cap?" a trapper named Warrington asked.

"Looks to me like another one of them *incidents,* boys. Reckon it must have been those damned Americans again," Smythe replied straight-faced, shaking his shaggy head in mock sadness.

Some of the trappers chuckled, others held back

15

their true feelings, for every man there understood that to steer a course across the bow of this old mountain pirate was to invite the Grim Reaper to dinner.

> " 'A knight there was, and he a worthy man,
> Who, from the moment that he first began
> To ride about the world, loved chivalry,
> Truth, honor, freedom and all courtesy.' "

"Sounds like a right honorable fellow," Kit Carson said, nodding his head in approval. "I like that thar part about honor and freedom. What else does that book say about him, Gray Feather?"

Waldo Gray Feather Smith glanced up from the thick copy of Chaucer's *Canterbury Tales*, which he'd been reading from upon the gently rocking back of his pony, and said, "If you'd stop interrupting me, Kit, you'd know what else it says."

Kit glanced back, narrowing his keen blue eyes at the Ute's obvious rebuke. "Whal, pardon me all to blazes, Mr. Smith."

Waldo Gray Feather Smith—or simply Gray Feather, as Kit usually called his traveling companion—was born of a full-blooded Ute Woman and a very English-blooded American father. He'd lived the first half of his life with his mother's people in the Rocky Mountains, and the second half with his father's people in their great Cambridge home. The elder Smith, a wealthy merchant who had made a fortune in shipping on the Erie Canal, had thought it absolutely necessary that his only son receive a *proper* education—which, of course, for anyone living in Cambridge meant Harvard College.

Gray Feather had studied English literature, then

returned to the people of his youth to teach them English. But Chief Walkara had declared that English was not necessary for his people since he firmly believed that the Spanish were about to move north and take over the land.

Kit liked Gray Feather, but sometimes the Ute's impatience with Kit's simple, straightforward, and down-home ways rankled—just a little.

Gray Feather cleared his throat and continued:

" 'Full worthy was he in his liege-lord's war—' "

"Liege-lord? What the devil does that mean?"

Gray Feather lowered the book again for perhaps the tenth time since beginning the tale and glared at his traveling companion. Then his frown softened and he drew in a long, calming breath. "A liege-lord," he began patiently, "is someone to whom you owe an allegiance, Kit. In this case, it's the sovereign of the land. Our knight owes his allegiance to the king—his liege-lord—and he fights his wars. It's what's known as feudal law."

"Hmm. Sorta like President Jackson."

"Exactly. President Jackson would be the liege-lord and, say, Captain Philip St. George Cooke might be his knight. Understand?"

"I think I've got a handle on it, Gray Feather," Kit replied, bristling at the Ute's condescending tone.

"Good. Now, may I continue, or do you not want to hear any more?"

"You're doing just fine thar. Don't let me stop you."

" 'And therein had he ridden (none more far)

17

As well in Christendom as heathenesse,
And honored everywhere for—' ''

"Heathen*esse*? Is that a real word?"

Gray Feather lowered the book just enough to glower over the top of it. A strained calmness was in his voice when he said, "Yes, it is. It's Middle English. It refers to the manners and customs of the heathens."

"Bring that over here a minute and let me see it."

"See it? What good will that do? You can't read."

Kit reined his horse to a stop and waited for Gray Feather to pull up alongside him.

"There." The Indian's finger stabbed at the page. "Heathen-*esse*. Heathenesse."

"So, that's the way it looks all written out on paper. How do you reckon I can remember what it looks like and what it means, Gray Feather?"

"The easiest way I know of to remember its meaning is to use the word a few times in some sentences. As far as remembering how it looks, well, it might just be easier if I teach you the rudiments of phonics. That way you can sound out any word you come across."

"Phonics? Sounds like Arapaho."

"Actually, it's from the French, who borrowed it from Latin. Try making up a sentence using the word."

Kit thought a moment, then looked Gray Feather in the eye and said, "All right, how about this: The wild Comanche scalped the *heathenesse* Ute with his butcher knife."

Gray Feather grimaced. "I suppose that's one way to use the word, although that's not the precise meaning of the word. Why not give it another try, Kit?''

Kit Carson rocked back in his saddle and studied the matter some. Then his view came back to Gray Feather and his sharp, blue eyes narrowed. ''When his powder run out, the trapper stood thar in the midst of Walkara's *heathenesse* warriors, wheeling his rifle like Samson done with the jawbone of an ass, busting skulls right and left.''

Gray Feather's frown lengthened. ''I'm beginning to see a pattern forming here,'' he commented dryly.

Inwardly, Kit was laughing. But to Gray Feather, he said straight-faced, ''Whal, is that closer to what you wanted to hear?''

''You know, Kit, I don't think your heart is really into learning how to read.''

''Oh? What makes you think that?''

''You are approaching the subject with a rather frivolous attitude. You are not giving it the diligence you give to other tasks. When you take on a job, such as carrying a message from Jim Bridger to Major Collins like you are now, you are all business. When your are tracking man or beast your attention is riveted. When you barter at the rendezvous for supplies you are masterful. When it comes to fighting there is none better. And as far as shooting goes, I've watched you spend hours practicing with that rifle of yours, shooting pinecones off a rock at a hundred and fifty yards. But when it comes to reading, well, you treat it as of little consequence. I don't understand you, Kit.''

Kit glanced at the long J. J. Henry rifle cradled in the crook of his arm. It was constructed after the Lancaster pattern, and although the stock was badly scarred, and patched about the wrist with rawhide where it had developed a crack, the rifle was a good one—a 32-gauge buffalo gun that shot as true as an honorable man's word. He thought of the dispatch from Bridger to be delivered to Colonel Collins, which he was carrying in his hunting bag. It contained a map of the caches of skins and gunpowder that Bridger had left for the Colonel to collect on his way down from the north country where he and a party of men had been trapping the dangerous Blackfoot country. Then he glanced at Gray Feather.

"Reckon you're right, Gray Feather. Readin' words on a paper is fine if you know how to do it, but out here it just isn't all that important. Not like those other things you mentioned. A man can survive without knowing how to read a single word. But if that man has no gunpowder, or he can't track or shoot straight, or he barters for less lead, blankets, or foo-faraws to trade with the Injuns than he's a-goin' to need to carry him through the season, chances are that man will end up buried in this here untamed country."

"Just the same, I know that you do want to learn how to read."

"I'll admit it. And someday I will." There had been several times when reading would have come in handy, and a few times when the handicap had proved an embarrassment to him. But still, it wasn't high on his list of things to do.

"Well, do you want me to keep reading?"

"That's another thing. The story's got my interest up, and I'd like to hear more, but this here is Injun country that we're riding through, and reading aloud makes a mite more noise than I'm comfortable with." Kit looked over. "I would have mentioned it earlier,

20

but didn't want to hurt your feelings, Gray Feather."

"Indian country? It's Flathead country!"

"I know that. And I know the Flatheads are one of the friendliest tribes about. But just the same, I don't like announcing our comings and goings to the world."

Gray Feather grinned. "I wouldn't be concerned about the Flatheads. I know a few of them personally. In fact, I have a very close friend, Man With Many Horses, who has recently married a Flathead girl and moved in with her tribe. Man With Many Horses and I grew up together before I left my people and moved east."

"I didn't know Utes married Flatheads."

"It happens sometimes. You know, we *heathenesse* savages aren't always fighting each other."

Kit gave a short laugh. Then all at once he reined to a halt, staring hard at something ahead.

"What's the matter?" Gray Feather asked, coming instantly alert.

Kit pointed at a dark smudge in the sky.

Gray Feather squinted. "What is it?"

"Crows. Thar, circling over something."

The Ute shook his head. "You never cease to amaze me. I'd have never seen them."

"Whal, that's because you've trained your eyes to look no farther than the book at the end of your arm. This is a big country, and if you wait until danger's only two feet away before you notice it, it's likely to be too late."

Gray Feather grimaced. "Circling crow can mean only one thing. There's something dead over there."

21

"Or dying," Kit added ominously.

His curiosity aroused, Kit Carson turned his horse off the trail and started in the direction of the wheeling birds.

Chapter Two

The sun had inched but a few degrees across the sky when Kit came upon the trail of a large party. There were several prints of shod horses among the smaller, open-hoof pony prints. It was plain to the mountain man that this was a company of trappers leading a string of packhorses. A couple of moments spent hunkered down over the prints quickly told Kit that there were perhaps ten men in all and half a dozen pack animals, some carrying very heavy loads.

Back in the saddle, Kit and Gray Feather moved silently, following the meandering path of a mountain stream. The sight of an elk carcass brought Kit to stop, and when he strolled back to his horse, shaking his head, Gray Feather asked what was wrong.

"Whoever shot it just let it lay," Kit said, puzzled.

23

"The animal might have run off after it was shot and the hunter couldn't find it."

Kit shook his head, removed his black beaver slouch hat, and wiped the sweat from its band. "No, there was no blood on its fur. Whoever shot it dropped it in its tracks. Maybe something scared him off before he could take the meat?"

"The Flatheads?"

Kit frowned, then shook his head, still puzzled. "I reckon anything is possible."

But the mystery deepened a quarter of a mile farther when the carcass of a blacktail was discovered. Like the elk, it had not been butchered.

"Someone could be shooting them just for the sport of it," Gray Feathered concluded.

"Maybe," Kit allowed grudgingly, then shook his head. "But I don't think so. Men of the mountains don't tote along enough powder and lead to be shooting it off frivolously. Killing game for sport and not at least taking the tenderloin and liver just isn't like them."

They continued to follow the trail. Suddenly Kit reined to a halt again and sniffed the air. The circling crows were nearly overhead now, just beyond a stand of trees, cawing and diving out of the sky at something beyond.

"You smell that?"

Gray Feather screwed up his lips and wrinkled his nose. "I might not be as observant as you, Kit, but my nose works just fine. I've smelled that kind of death before."

"So have I."

The two men pushed on through the trees. An explosion of black feathers scattered for the sky, screaming down at them and roiling overhead like an angry storm cloud.

Immediately the putrid smell of rotting flesh engulfed them. Kit's horse shied away, but he held it there as he surveyed the bowl of black mud, most of five acres' worth, Kit reckoned, measuring it by the line the water had left behind. It had once been a big beaver dam, from the looks of it, but it had been drained dry in what must have amounted to only a few hours. What had been left behind was nearly the entire fish population, which now lay shriveled up and baking under a hot sun. The pond was still muddy, but already it had begun to dry.

The crows came back, lighting on dead fish all around them. "Now we know," Gray Feather said in a nasal tone, trying not to breathe in any more of the horrible odor than necessary.

Kit urged his horse across the drying bottom.

"Where you going?" Gray Feather asked.

"I want to take a look at the dam."

"Look? You can see what happened. It burst!"

Kit rode along the muddy edge, away from the flowing creek, which was busily cutting itself a new channel through the accumulated silt. How many years this area had been inundated Kit had no way of judging, but he couldn't help imagining that this might have been how the earth looked to Noah the day he opened up that ark and stepped outside. And the smell might have been similar, too. But then, being locked away with all those animals for a year or so, it might have been a welcome relief from the smell *inside* that ark!

As he rode, crows scattered before him, only to settle again in his wake when he had passed. Kit grinned. It reminded him of another biblical story his mother had read to him as a child: that of the Red Sea parting before Moses and the Israelites, only to close up on the Egyptians behind them. At the beaver dam he dismounted and walked along its top to the place, about midway across, where it had given way.

Gray Feather came along a little behind him, scattering crows as the prow of a ship parts the water. His pony, its hooves caked in mud, seemed none too happy with the ordeal, but it plowed on with indomitable spirit anyway.

Kit was studying the break. "Come over here and look at this," he said when the Ute was close enough to step off onto the dam.

Gray Feather hunkered down next to him. "This place smells worse than an overused sweat lodge."

"Looky here. See this mark? It almost looks like someone used a long pole like a lever here."

Gray Feather glanced up, startled. "Are you suggesting that this was broken apart on purpose?"

Kit inclined his head to the next beaver dam down the valley. "That one's been busted open too."

"It burst from the outflow of this dam. That's not surprising, is it?"

Kit grunted. It wasn't how he read the signs. "Whal, let's you and me take a look and see."

They led their horses across the few hundred yards of grass that had been flattened by the torrent from the dam above. The lower pond had been smaller than the first, but had still held a sizable fish population, which was now filling the stomachs of the local birds. The dam had burst in the middle, like the first, but this time Kit spied something different.

"Hmm," he said, touching a gash in one of the

stout branches that had formed the dam.

"What did you find?"

Kit glanced up at his Indian partner. "Whal, Gray Feather, if this was Mother Nature's doings, she's taken to swinging an ax. Look here. This wood was sliced apart, and it was a good, sharp, steel ax what done it, judging from the clean cut."

Gray Feather stared at the wood. But before he could speak, Kit was bounding off in another direction. The mountain man had spied something wedged in the woven branches of the dam, about halfway from the top. Using a stout branch, he fished it out. An iron chain thunked to the muddy basin, pulling along with it the half-rotted carcass of a beaver with a steel spring trap still clamped solidly about its hind leg.

"Here's the one that got away from them," Kit said, turning the decayed remains over with his stick. "He managed to pull the chain loose and swim for his lodge, but he didn't quite make it. Drowned before he got thar. I'd say he's been dead two weeks."

"Then whoever did this must have done it less than two weeks ago."

Kit nodded. "They probably cleaned these ponds of every beaver they could trap, then busted the dams. Maybe no more than four or five days ago."

"But why?" Gray Feather puzzled.

"Why and *who*?" Kit added as he compressed the springs and levered the jaws of the trap open. "Now, this is curious." He showed the trap to the Indian. "What do you make of it?"

Gray Feather shrugged. "It's a beaver trap. What's curious about that?"

"It's a rat trap design. Size number four."

"So?"

"It's of British design. Used generally by the Hudson's Bay Company."

"Ah!" Gray Feather began to understand the implication of that. "Are you certain?"

Kit showed him the stamp in the steel. "Can you read that?"

"It says 'T. Moore.' "

"Moore? He's a smithy over at Fort Vancouver. If he made this trap, it only seems plain that one of the Fort's trapping brigades set it."

"That's all very interesting, Kit, but it still doesn't answer my question. Why would trappers from the Hudson's Bay Company destroy these beaver ponds?"

Kit shook his head. It didn't make sense to him either. Both the Americans and the British depended on the beaver for their livelihood. What could be gained by destroying the ponds where the beaver lived and bred?

Suddenly a great commotion of cawing birds shattered his thoughts as once again a cloud of black spiraled for the sky. Instantly Kit wheeled around, bringing his rifle to bear . . . and froze where he stood.

Kit had been so intent on figuring out the puzzle that he had been completely unaware of the fifteen armed warriors who had been easing their way toward them. It was only when the crows scattered that he had had any notion of them at all, and by then it was too late. There was no chance to run, and fighting was hopeless since every one of the warriors carried a musket. But they were Flathead Indians, and when Kit recognized them, he breathed a sigh of relief and lowered his rifle. The Flatheads were one of the few tribes that had accepted the white trappers and even welcomed them onto their lands.

These particular Flathead warriors, however, did not have a welcoming look on their scowling faces. It was more a look of murder, Kit lamented as they circled in on all sides and his brief bubble of relief deflated into a hard lump of alarm that settled like a sack of lead shot in the pit of his stomach.

The sudden flurry of birds wheeling skyward that had taken place when Kit and Gray Feather first came upon the shattered beaver ponds had alerted Two Bulls and the war party he led. Perhaps the enemy who had snuck into their country had been discovered, he thought. They had not been far from the beaver ponds, and altering their course, they had arrived even as Kit and Gray Feather had been studying the steel trap.

"These two have come back for the iron jaws," Two Bulls surmised. "The iron jaws that catch the beaver are too valuable for them to lose even one."

"This will be their undoing," Soaring Hawk whispered at his side as the other warriors quietly dismounted and crept to the forest's edge.

"If we move swiftly, we can surround them. Then I will have their lives for the lives of our brothers." Two Bulls's fist tightened around his musket, then, drawing back its heavy hammer, he checked to see that the pan beneath the flint still held its priming powder.

"Should we not take them prisoners instead, Two Bulls?"

These words of moderation came from a man whom Two Bulls had always considered an outsider and an interloper. An impatient snarl moved across Two Bulls's lips. "You have the courage of a woman, Man With Many Horses," he hissed.

Undaunted, Man With Many Horses said quietly, "But if you are wrong, then we will have killed innocent men."

"Wrong!" Two Bulls thrust a finger at the strangers. "Look, they have returned for their property. How could they not be the Americans that have entered our land and have murdered our brothers?"

Some of the warriors nodded in agreement. Others wanted to hear Man With Many Horses out.

"If they are the evildoers, then all the more reason to take them prisoners. Alive, they can tell us where the others have gone. Dead, they can tell us nothing."

In spite of his hatred for Man With Many Horses, Two Bulls saw the wisdom in what he said. Many of the warriors agreed.

"We will capture them, and afterward I will decide if they are to be killed or taken back to the village."

"Calling Elk would want to question them," Man With Many Horses advised.

Most of the warriors agreed that their chief *would* wish to do so.

An impatient scowl creased Two Bulls's dark face. He didn't like to have his decisions overruled, even if it was for the best. And he detested men who forced a change to his plans. In particular he hated the outsider, Man With Many Horses, who had more than once crossed his path.

Giving a signal, Two Bulls led the warriors out of the cover of the forest and down toward the muddy remains of the beaver pond. They made it as far as the empty pond's edge without the trappers noticing, so intent were they upon examining the trap. Then the birds exploded into the sky before them. . . .

In an instant the Flatheads rushed forward, brandishing their London Fusils. Seeing themselves surrounded, the two trappers put up their weapons. Two Bulls ordered his men to take their rifles, tomahawks, and knives, and only after he had disarmed the trappers did he discover that one of them was an Indian!

"Gray Feather! Is it you?"

The man who had spoken pushed his way to the front of the warriors circling the trappers. He was a tall warrior and well-built. He somehow stood apart from the rest, although Kit could not decide exactly what it was about the fellow that made him different.

Kit was perplexed by this unprompted attack, and his attention remained focused on the muskets and scowling faces that stared back at him.

Gray Feather's head came instantly around, searching for the man who had spoken his name. At length his view fell upon the tall warrior. The Ute's eyes compressed slightly, wonderingly, and then suddenly sprung wide.

"Man With Many Horses?"

"Yes, it is I, brother," the warrior said, slipping immediately into the Ute tongue. "My heart is both gladdened and saddened that it should be you here, friend of my youth."

That sounded ominous to Kit as he pondered this hostile change in the Flatheads' attitudes. Every one he had ever met had been at least tolerant of the white trappers, if not downright friendly.

"In truth, it does *my* heart good to discover you

31

among these warriors. I thought for certain Kit and I were going to lose our scalps.''

Man With Many Horses glanced at Kit Carson, then back at Gray Feather, the spontaneous look of surprise and joy suddenly fading from his face. "And the truth is, I fear, that you may yet still give your scalp over to Two Bulls, to add to those which already hang from his lodge poles.''

"Enough of this talk!'' the leader barked. "You know these men, interloper?'' He spoke the Flathead tongue, which Kit understood only slightly, it being a dialect of the Salishan language and spoken mainly in the Northwest, a part of the frontier in which Kit had not yet spent much time.

"I know one of them,'' Man With Many Horses replied tightly. "A friend of my youth.''

The leader's scowl deepened. He barked orders for the warriors to close in around Kit and Gray Feather. With vicious jabs from the barrels of the warriors' muskets, Kit and Gray Feather began moving.

Where they were being taken, Kit had no way of knowing, and when he asked, even Gray Feather's friend was closemouthed. All Kit knew was that they were heading north in the company of Indians who were of a mighty unfriendly state of mind . . . which didn't help to put his own state of mind at rest.

Chapter Three

The march lasted an hour or so. Kit felt as if he were in the midst of a swarm of hornets the whole way. He ached in a dozen places where an impatient musket muzzle had urged him on, even though he and Gray Feather were keeping right up with the Flatheads. After the fourth or fifth jab he reckoned that the prodding was just their way of venting some pent-up anger. Kit suspected that a scalping would have provided the relief they sought, but something was keeping them from it.

"Whal, so much for us being in *friendly* Injun country," Kit commented to Gray Feather at one point. The remark immediately brought the muzzle of one of the London Fusils—"Hudson's Bay Flukes," as the Americans sometimes called them—squarely against Kit's spine. He winced and scowled at the culprit, who merely scowled back twice as fiercely.

These warriors had all the firepower and Kit had none, so for the moment he had to bide his time. But he was keeping a tally of the abuses. *Soon, sometime soon,* he promised himself, soothing his rising ire, *will come my turn.*

The forest opened onto the sunny slope of a grassy plain where there stood at least thirty lodges of the Flathead village. Women, children, and men gathered around as the war party marched their prisoners through the village. Excited dogs romped alongside, greeting the returning warriors, who became more vicious with their prodding, as if putting on a show for the folks standing there watching. They shoved Kit and Gray Feather into the center of the village where a post the size of a small tree had been driven into the ground. The two trappers were tied to it, and the people gathered around them as if Kit and Gray Feather were a couple of curious critters from some faraway place, just like one Kit had once seen on display in a St. Louis storefront window.

As the warriors went off with wives and children at their sides, Man With Many Horses turned back and gave them a long, unhappy look. An attractive woman wearing a doeskin dress finely decorated with glass beads came up alongside the tall Ute warrior. He turned away, and they walked off together toward one of the lodges. Kit settled down for what he thought might prove to be a long wait—if for no other reason than that he reckoned being the center of attention would tend to make the time drag out.

"Think your friend will help us out of this fix?" Kit asked as the crowd began to disperse.

"He would if he could," Gray Feather answered glumly. "But Man With Many Horses is an outsider.

He has only recently married into this village, and as such his words carry little weight.''

''What's got them all riled up?'' Kit wondered aloud, studying the village. He was struck by the prosperity he saw everywhere. British trade muskets abounded, as did colorful, very expensive Hudson's Bay blankets. ''These people must be doing right well for themselves, hunting and trapping and trading with the King George men.''

''Better than most I've seen,'' Gray Feather agreed.

A fly buzzed near Kit's ear. With his hands tied, the best Kit could do was shake his head. But it was a minor annoyance. The blazing sun overhead was far more bothersome, and after a few hours of roasting without anyone offering them a drink, Kit felt certain his brains were frying. Throughout the afternoon the village ignored them. A dog curled up nearby for a while, but after a few minutes the heat drove it off to the shade of one of the lodges. Only the flies seemed unaffected.

Kit closed his eyes against the relentless glare, trying to ignore the sweat trickling into his eyes and the salty taste it left at the corners of his mouth. He recalled his trip across the burning desert to California a few years earlier; the line of staggering men and animals that stretched for almost a mile along the burning trail. And he remembered the sight and smell of water, and the mad rush of men and beasts to the small, life-giving pool that he had finally discovered. He could taste it again, but when he licked his dry lips, all he got was the sting of salt upon his tongue.

The sun dropped low to the west and shadows lengthened. Shade from a nearby lodge stretched out to offer some welcome relief to Kit and Gray Feather.

In a little while a man emerged from a dwelling. Three braves, all younger than he, walked at his side as he came over and hovered above the two trappers. Two Bulls was one of them, and the two others were braves from the party of warriors who had taken them captive.

"I am Elk Calling, chief of the Beaver Lodge Clan," the older man said in good English.

Kit blinked the sweat from his eyes and moistened his lips. "My name is Kit Carson. My partner here is Gray Feather. Why have your braves taken us captive and bound us in your village? Thar's always been peace between the whites and the Flatheads."

"You have come onto the lands of my people bringing death. It is not Elk Calling or the People who have broken the peace which our peoples have had."

The chief's accusation snapped Kit's half-fried brain from its lethargy. "What have we done to your people? What death?" he demanded.

Two Bulls said bitterly, "Do you think we are fools?" His English was not as good as the chief's, but there was no doubting the passion behind his words . . . or the poison. "You of the American companies come through our land, killing the game and breaking up the beaver's home so that he will no longer live in our land."

"Wagh! What are you talkin' about? Gray Feather and me, we're just passing through. We've taken no more game than we needed to live."

"That is a lie—"

Calling Elk stopped Two Bulls from further accusations and said to Kit, "You were found on the place where beavers once made their lodges. Do you deny this?"

"No, I don't deny it. But we was only—"

Calling Elk threw up a hand to silence Kit. "And you held the iron jaws that catch the beaver. Do you deny this?"

Kit tried to stand, but the leather thongs holding him to the post were too short and yanked him back. "We came upon the place because the great flock of birds caught our eye. Whoever busted up that beaver dam did it before we got there. And the trap was something I'd just found. We'd never seen it before."

"He lies. I see it in his eyes," Two Bulls charged, glancing to the other two warriors for support. Eagerly, they nodded their heads in agreement.

Gray Feather said, "What Kit is telling you is the truth. We are only passing through."

Calling Elk shifted his dark eyes toward the Ute. "I might believe you, for your people and my people have not been enemies. If you were Blackfoot, I would have had you killed at once. But as to the truth of this matter, I am slow to judge. Perhaps you two have not done these things, but it is the American companies who have killed many warriors, and many deer and elk. They have hurt the land much. The deaths of our young men at the Americans' hands can mean only war between the Beaver Lodge Clan and the Americans."

"Chief Calling Elk," Kit said, his thoughts racing ahead, trying to make some sense of what the chief had said, "I don't know what's all been a-goin' on here, seeing as we're just passing through carrying a message to our brothers in the north country where your ancient enemies, the Blackfeet, make their lodges. But I can tell you this: No American trapper that I know of would do the things you said."

37

"I would expect to hear no less from this white man," Two Bulls growled. "Calling Elk, give me the honor of cutting the forked tongue from his lying mouth."

"But it's true!" Gray Feather blurted with rising concern in his voice. "There must be some mistake."

Two Bulls jerked his knife from its sheath, but Calling Elk reached out and stayed his hand. "You have the passion of youth, Two Bulls, but this matter is one for thoughtfulness, not emotion. These men are going nowhere, and there is still much time left for sending them on to the dwelling places of their ancestors."

"Chief of our people. May I add my words to those which have already been spoken here?"

Calling Elk glanced over as the tall Ute came through the small gathering of warriors and stood before him. Man With Many Horses displayed a confidence that some men just naturally radiated. His height, his broad, muscular chest, his handsomely chiseled face, his quiet confidence, all worked together to lend a presence that overshadowed the smaller, angrier warrior who still clutched a knife in his fist.

Kit did not know what Two Bulls had against this man, but it was obvious that the shorter warrior detested the Ute. Perhaps it was the Ute's self-assuredness, perhaps jealousy over the way in which God had chosen to fashion each man—one tall and handsome, the other short and always brooding—that stirred Two Bulls' wrath . . . or perhaps it was something else altogether.

The chief inclined his head and said, "Since joining with our people, you have served this clan honorably. Your bravery is without question, and you have kept your place and have observed our traditions, which is fitting for one new to our ways. You may speak.''

"Thank you, Grandfather," Man With Many Horses began, using the term of respect toward an older man that, Kit noted, had been distinctly lacking in Two Bulls's manner of addressing the chief. "As you have said, I am new to this village, and have much to learn, but over the last two winters I have come to know and love the people of my wife as if they were my own people. Now I consider them *my* people, wise chief. But still I cannot forget the people of my youth, for they will always be bound to my heart.''

Man With Many Horses looked at the two men tied helplessly to the post. "I do not know this white man, but I have met many like him before. My people, as have your people, have chosen to live in peace with them. And like you, I have known some who are good men, and some not good. But then, we can say the same thing of men of our own village.''

Although Man With Many Horses did not obviously indicate it, Kit felt certain that last remark had been a jab at Two Bulls, who was still scowling.

"This I already know," Calling Elk commented. "Are you speaking in their defense?''

"I am speaking in defense of the man called Gray Feather.''

Gray Feather stirred uneasily at Kit's side.

"Continue, then.''

"Gray Feather and I grew up together, in the mountains far to the south, from the place where the warm winds come and chases Old Man Frost back to his winter lodge. Our mothers are cousins. For twelve winters and summers we lived as close as brothers of the same lodge. Then his father, who lived far away in the land of the whites, where the sun brings the morning light, came and took him away, and I have seen my brother but only three times in all the winters he was gone. Then Gray Feather returned to the village of my people two winters ago with a white man called Kit Carson. My mother has told me this. Our chief, Walkara, knows this man, Carson, and trusts him. I know Gray Feather and trust him. We know that white trappers of the American companies have come onto our lands to make mischief and bring death to some of our young warriors, but I know in my heart that these two men are innocent.''

''You cannot know that, interloper!'' Two Bulls burst out. ''We caught them in the midst of their treachery.''

Calling Elk considered this a moment. ''Was it not a flight of birds that guided you to the broken beaver lodges, Two Bulls?''

''Yes, it was,'' the warrior admitted with a hint of caution in his voice that did not escape Kit's keen ears.

The chief nodded his head. ''And these two trappers say they were led there by a flight of birds as well.''

''So?''

''So perhaps, as Man With Many Horses has said, they are innocent.''

''You believe him?'' Two Bulls's voice rose in amazement.

''I believe only that these two may have found the

broken lodges as they claim—the same way that you found them—and before I have them killed, I wish to hear more." The chief glanced at the knife that Two Bulls had not yet returned to its sheath. "Cut the thongs that hold them."

"Me?"

"Your knife already waits in your hand, Two Bulls."

"It waits only for the pleasure of cutting out their hearts!" Thrusting the knife back into his belt, he turned and strode angrily away, with the two other warriors close on his heels.

Kit drew in a long sigh of relief as one of the other men did the chief's bidding. In a moment the thongs parted and fell away. Standing and rubbing circulation back into his hands, Kit said, "You made the right decision, Chief Calling Elk."

The older man merely grunted. It was plain that Calling Elk was still not as convinced of Kit's and Gray Feather's innocence as was Man With Many Horses.

Kit frowned. "Can we have our horses and property back?" he asked, thinking mainly of the dispatch that Jim Bridger had entrusted to him, and also that with their rifles in hand, an escape might be likely.

"No. All of that which was taken from you will remain in my lodge. If you two leave the village, I will have you killed. That will please Two Bulls, and I am not anxious to please him, so do not try to leave." Glancing at the tall Ute, Calling Elk continued, "Since you have vouched for these men, they will stay in your lodge until I have decided what must be done with them. They are in your charge. See that they remain there and that you do not do this people a dishonor, Man With Many Horses.''

''I will not dishonor our people, Grandfather. I will not let them leave.''

''Good.'' The chief turned and walked back to his lodge without further comment.

Man With Many Horses grimaced, and with a glance at the two trappers he wheeled away and started for his lodge. A quick look around the village told Kit that the alert warriors standing about with their London Fusils at the ready effectively eliminated any hope of escape—at least for the moment.

''Looks like we're staying for a while,'' Kit murmured to his friend.

''At least we are no longer bound,'' Gray Feather commented, taking an optimistic outlook.

''I reckon that's something,'' Kit agreed soberly as he and Gray Feather followed the warrior.

Chapter Four

"Reckon we owe you our lives, Man With Many Horses. Thanks for speaking up for us," Kit said as they sat around the small fire that burned in the center of the warrior's lodge.

The tall Indian who sat across the fire from him, packing the bowl of his pipe with tobacco, narrowed a dark eye at the mountain man. "I hope my trust has not been placed on shaking ground."

"How can you even think that?" Gray Feather asked. "We had nothing to do with destroying those beaver ponds."

"And the deer and elk that have been shot, and the warriors murdered?"

"That's preposterous! What reason could we have to do such a barbaric thing? You know me better than that!" Indignation burned in Gray Feather's voice.

Man With Many Horses grinned. "Since leaving

to live with the people of your father, you have begun to talk strangely, my old friend.''

Kit gave a short laugh. ''Gray Feather is the oddest-talking Injun I've ever run across. He's got words in him big enough to choke a buffler.''

Gray Feather fell into a brooding silence, but whether it was caused by Man With Many Horses's veiled accusations, or from his gibe at the Ute's extensive eastern education, Kit could not tell. Just then the open doorway darkened and a woman stepped inside. She was beautiful; her smile nearly took Kit's breath away. She was the same woman he had seen with this tall warrior earlier that morning.

''This is my wife, Mary Fawn Hiding.''

''Mary?'' Kit said, surprised. ''That doesn't sound much like a Flathead name.''

Mary Fawn Hiding smiled. ''It is a name my father, Tall Bear, once heard from the black-robed men who came to our village many winters ago to tell us of the God of white man.''

Mary Fawn Hiding was a captivating beauty with long raven hair, unblemished skin, and a smile that lit up the dim lodge as if a window had suddenly been cut into it to allow the sunlight to stream in. Her husband being the ruggedly handsome fellow that he was, Kit reckoned that between the two of them they would one day raise a passel of right handsome tykes.

Man With Many Horses went on to introduce his boyhood friend. ''This is Gray Feather. I have told you about him. He and I grew up together. Our mothers are cousins.''

''I have heard much about you, Gray Feather,'' she said. ''You are the one they used to call Little Mending Woman?''

44

Gray Feather groaned softly and frowned. Kit had never seen an Indian blush before.

"Little Mending Woman?" Kit grinned. "You never told me that."

Gray Feather winced and said to Man With Many Horses, "Thanks for telling everyone about that?"

Mary Fawn Hiding averted her eyes. "I'm sorry. It is something you did not wish to speak about?"

The embarrassed Ute shrugged his shoulders. "Well, now that it's out in the open," he speared Man With Many Horses with an accusatory stare, "I suppose I ought to tell you all exactly what *did* happen, just so that you get the story straight."

Man With Many Horses said in his defense, "I have only told my wife because the incident holds such fond memories."

"For some, maybe," Gray Feather noted dourly.

Kit said, "Whal, let's hear the tale."

"It really isn't much of a tale, Kit, except that when the tale is told over and over again, it becomes more than it was. I think I was eleven or twelve, I'm not certain. It was shortly before my father came to take me back east. All the young boys were going to go hunting with the older warriors of the tribe. Sort of like going to school to learn your lessons, only in our case, the schoolhouse was the wide outdoors, and the lessons were in setting deadfalls, tracking, skinning—you know, the kinds of skills needed to survive.

"Well, I've always been a little different from the other boys, and I suspect it was because half of me was white. I was fascinated by everything, but particularly by the intricate patterns the women were able to weave into the baskets they made, and the stitchery of porcupine quills and glass beads. I don't know why I found it fascinating, I just did. Of course, anything considered woman's work was eschewed by the other boys.''

''Whoa, back up thar, Gray Feather. What was that word you just said?'' Kit asked.

''Eschewed?''

''Yep, that's the one. Are we all talking the same language here?''

''It means to shun or avoid.'' Gray Feather saw the confusion in Man With Many Horses's and his wife's face as well, and translated the word into the Salishan tongue, then went on. ''This particular hunting trip was my—and Man With Many Horses's, who was called Little Wanderer back then—second or third time, and we were both excited, but on the way out, I suddenly remembered my lance, which I'd left behind. We were about a quarter of a mile from the village, so the men agreed to wait while I ran back to fetch it.

''Well, as fate would have it, right there in front of my mother's tepee were a group of women and many of the girls of the tribe learning their lessons. In other words, the women were teaching the girls all about decorating a skin shirt with porcupine quills. I grabbed up the lance, but on the way out paused just a moment to watch the sewing lessons. I became entranced, of course, by the skill of my mother's fingers and by the lovely beadwork she was producing, and forgot all about the men and boys waiting for me outside the village. That is, until one of the men came back looking for me only to discover me hunched down beside a girl cousin, completely absorbed by what they were doing.''

"After that, everyone called Gray Feather 'Little Mending Woman,' " Man With Many Horses finished.

"Needless to say, I never lived down that embarrassment and when my father came to take me away, I was anxious to go with him."

After the laughter died down—and Gray Feather had been laughing too—Kit moved the conversation on to his more immediate concern. Calling Elk had made some serious accusations, and had taken all their gear, including the important dispatch to Major Collins. Without their weapons, blankets, flints, and fire-striking tools, Kit knew they'd have a devil of a time making it back to civilization.

"What's been happening here, Man With Many Horses? Why have the Flatheads turned against the trappers?"

"Not against all the trappers," the Ute said thoughtfully, "only those who trap for the American companies. We have no fight with the men of the Hudson's Bay Company."

"We have always had peace between our peoples."

"The breaking of the peace is by the white man. Not the Indian."

"How so?" Gray Feather asked.

Man With Many Horses looked at his old friend. "The American trappers have come onto our lands and have broken many of the beavers' lodges. They have killed much game, too, but more than that, they have murdered many of our warriors and taken their scalps."

"That don't sound like any trappers I've known," Kit said. "Oh, thar might be one or two of a cantankerous nature who might do what you claim, but they're called renegades and they don't last long among the mountain men, and that's a fact.''

"You speak true-sounding words, Kit Carson, but my eyes have seen what they have done."

"How can you be certain it was the Americans? Thar are plenty of British and Canadians in these parts."

Man With Many Horses shook his head. "No, the British and Canadians have been at peace with our people long before the Americans. It is the British who have traded many guns for the beaver we catch."

"I've noticed," Kit commented. "Thar must be a hundred London Fusils in camp."

"They know the trouble we face. They have lowered their price on guns and blankets, so that if the time comes, we might fight the Americans and win."

This was beginning to sound ominous. "You said you have seen these things with your own eyes?"

"I have seen the game lying dead, and the beaver lodges broken apart, and the bodies of three of our warriors have been discovered."

"Did you find them?"

Man With Many Horses shook his head again. "No, I only saw their bodies when the trapper, Smythe, brought them into the village. His men found them."

"Smythe? Who is this man?"

"Smythe is chief of the trappers from Fort Vancouver."

"One of King George's men. And he told you the men were killed by Americans?"

"He brought back rifles and knives which had been lost in the battle. They are all American. And the traps he has found have been American too.''

''Sounds mighty circumstantial to me,'' Gray Feather noted.

''Sounds like we got big trouble brewing unless we can get to the bottom of this and run down these renegades.'' Kit thought a moment. ''Can you show me these rifles and traps?''

''Calling Elk has them. I do not think he would show them to you. There is much anger toward the white man now. You must be looked fondly upon by the gods, or Two Bulls would have killed you at once this morning. I would not want to tempt them any further today.''

''Two Bulls seems particularly cantankerous.''

Man With Many Horses frowned. ''Two Bulls has much to be angry about.'' He cast a brief glance toward his wife, then looked back at Kit. ''His brother was the first brave to be murdered by the Americans. Two Bulls has been beating the war drums ever since. Calling Elk has resisted his urgings so far. He is a thoughtful man and knows what war will mean to this village. We have many guns, but the Americans have many more guns, and they have many young men who come from the place where the morning sun rises. As many as the buffalo; more than can be counted. But I fear that if another warrior falls to the Americans' guns, there can be no more hope for peace.''

Kit's lips tightened, thinning to a single, hard line. ''Whal, that might explain what Two Bulls has against me, and even Gray Feather thar, because he travels in my company, but it don't explain what he's got against you, Man With Many Horses, and it's plain as brass tacks that he hates you something fierce.''

Man With Many Horses glanced at the woman seated nearby him, and slowly his hand moved to grasp hers. "Yes, he hates me. It is because his desires were for Mary Fawn Hiding, but I won her heart. For this reason he hates me. The village knows this, and that is why no one pays him much attention when he flings false accusations at me. I have proven myself to the people, to the chief, and most important, to my wife. But even so, Two Bulls continues to undermine me at every turn in the path.''

Now Mary Fawn Hiding spoke up. "He would kill my husband if he could find a way to do so without bringing disgrace and banishment upon himself. But if he thinks I would go with him if my husband was with the ghosts of our ancestors, he has badly deceived himself.''

Kit grimaced. "Whal, my experience is that a man would do most anything to win the hand of the woman he loved. I'd not let that rascal Two Bulls come up on my blind side if I was you, Man With Many Horses.''

The warrior gave a short laugh. "I have eyes that see all around. Two Bulls will have to be much cleverer than he has proven to be so far if he wants to defeat Man With Many Horses.''

The tall Ute gave another laugh, fished a crackling twig from the fire, and put it to the pipe he had prepared. After getting it burning, he drew in a long smoke and passed it around to his left, to Gray Feather. Before it had reached Kit, a commotion outside brought them at once to their feet. Kit was out the door first. He drew up, startled, at what met his eye.

Three white trappers had ridden into the Flathead village, leading two horses loaded with something hidden beneath blankets. The leader was a burly man with a patch over one eye and a peg fastened below the knee of his right leg. The other two were both younger men, dressed in buckskins, carrying long rifles in the crooks of their arms. The chief came out of his lodge as braves closed in around the white men.

"Who are they?" Kit asked Man With Many Horses.

"The big man with much hair on his face, like a bear, is named Alexander Smythe. The two others with him are Wilber Port and Aston Marsten."

"Smythe? The fellow you was telling us about? Captain of a fur brigade out of Fort Vancouver?"

"Yes, that is the man."

Kit couldn't make out what the packhorses were carrying. More trade goods, he reckoned at first. Then he heard the brigade leader speak.

"Chief Calling Elk," Smythe said in an unmistakable British accent. "It is good to visit your village again. But I'm afraid I do not carry good news." As he spoke he happened to spy Kit. For a long moment the big man's single eye held Kit in a hard stare. "I see you've got one of them Americans here with you, Chief."

Calling Elk nodded his head, his dark eyes grave, his lips tight. "What is the news you bring to me, Alexander Smythe?"

The burly man winced and returned his view to the chief as more braves gathered around. Some made a move toward the packhorses. Smythe said, "At least

51

you've got one of them blackguards in your clutches. Don't let him get away. The Americans have been up to no good again, Chief.'' He glanced at the man called Port and nodded his head. Port slid off his saddle and took a knife to the ropes keeping the blankets in place.

They fell away, revealing the bodies beneath. A startled gasp arose from the men gathered there.

"It is Many Arrows and Swift Water Running!'' one of the warriors cried out.

"Sorry to have to bring them to you like this, Chief.'' Smythe frowned and shook his head. "Me and my men come across them a few miles back. It was a bloody mess, it was. When we got there they'd already been killed and scalped. But one of them managed to get ahold of this Green River knife from the American devil who murdered him.'' Smythe handed the damning evidence over to Calling Elk.

The chief stared at the knife with rage slowly rising like the head of steam in a paddle-wheeler's boilers. There was a sudden electricity in the air, like the coming of a mighty thunderstorm, as dozens of warriors closed in about the two bodies.

The hairs at the nape of Kit's neck began to rise, and with them a sinking feeling that when the gathering storm finally did explode, he knew exactly where the first bolt of lightning was going to strike!

Chapter Five

Glancing nervously around the Flathead encampment, Kit watched the village warriors swarm toward their chief and Smythe's men. With the angry mumbling moving through the throng, it was only a matter of moments before their rage turned into action. And with the people in a frenzy over the death of two of their villagers, there'd be no reprieve for Kit or Gray Feather this time.

Man With Many Horses remained at Gray Feather's side, but as the bodies of his adopted brothers were removed from the horses it was clear that his loyalties were torn. Kit wondered if Man With Many Horses's confidence in his old friend's innocence was waning. It appeared on the surface, even to Kit, who didn't want to believe it, that Americans *were* truly responsible for these deeds.

A small window of opportunity still remained open

to the two trappers, but it was quickly slamming shut. Kit had always been a firm believer in following one's instincts. In the past his spontaneous decisions had generally flown in the face of all logic, and often thrust his life onto the teetering edge of destruction. But each time Kit had somehow managed to leap out of the frying pan a few moments before his hide had begun to sizzle too badly.

Taking a casual step backward, Kit caught Gray Feather's eye. He gave him an almost imperceptible nod of his head and inclined his chin toward the line of trees that marked the forest's edge not very far beyond the village. Gray Feather returned the subtle signal. Kit caught his breath. With the swiftness of a panther, he snatched the knife from the sheath in Man With Many Horses's waistband and, bringing the hilt around, delivered a stunning blow to the tall warrior's midsection. The man crumpled. Kit heard a startled cry from Mary Fawn Hiding, but by that time he and Gray Feather were in flight. The lodges swept past and then they were in the open. Every fiber in Kit's body was taut, waiting for the punch of a bullet or the report of a musket.

The forest was almost upon them when the first shot rang out. Kit flinched as the bullet whistled past his ear. Two more gunshots, followed a moment later by half a dozen more. But by then the first of the trees had closed in behind them. A chunk of bark exploded to Kit's right, the thud of lead against wood *whoomp*ed off another.

Fleeing through the sparse growth toward the thicker timber that lay beyond, Kit ran a zigzagging course, hoping to thwart their aim. But already some of the immediate dread was lifting from his shoulders.

Any hit this far out would be by sheer accident, since the Indians' unrifled muskets could shoot straight for only forty or fifty yards. Kit and Gray Feather were already far beyond that by now—and Kit knew that few men could run and load a musket and shoot it with any accuracy all at the same time.

"Kit!" Gray Feather cried out.

When the mountain man glanced back, his partner had stumbled, then caught himself against a tree. His hand clutched his side, and a crimson sheen was beginning to show between his fingers. Kit wheeled about and came up beside the Ute. Through the scattered trees he could still see the Flathead village— and the stream of warriors fanning out from it.

Kit thrust the knife he had taken under his belt and threw an arm around his friend. "Got to get moving. Hit bad?" he asked.

"I don't know," Gray Feather gasped between breaths. They crashed through thicker brush, and as the forest grew deeper, Kit shifted his course every few hundred feet. The tactic slowed them down some, but each shift would throw a stumbling block in the path of the Flatheads not far behind—or at least Kit hoped so. Alone, Kit could have easily eluded the warriors, but unless he could come up with some clever maneuver now, there really was little hope of escape so long as he remained with Gray Feather.

Kit could feel his friend slowing. He bore more of the Ute's weight upon his shoulder as they plunged wildly into the forest. Every step of the way his keen eyes were studying and assessing the terrain, his brain whirling and calling forth everything he had learned about following a trail . . . or about leaving one, as he and Gray Feather were doing now.

The land tilted unexpectedly, and Kit found himself suddenly backpedaling to keep the two of them from reeling headlong down the treacherously steep incline. Somewhere ahead he thought that he heard running water, and his nose confirmed it as the rush of cooler air from the valley below brought up with it the damp, unmistakable scent of moist ground.

A few moments later the land leveled out at the edge of a rushing mountain stream. The stream was not too wide, but it was deep. When Kit plunged in, the water rose nearly to his chest. The bottom was rocky and difficult to navigate. Kit considered pushing on right across it and continuing along the far side, but Gray Feather was rapidly losing strength.

Now, dodging into a river to elude pursuers was about as original as griddle cakes for breakfast. It was a trick old as the hills, if not older. But Kit figured that if he could only move downstream a few hundred yards without being spotted, he might be able to put a new twist to the ancient ploy.

The bank was heavily strewn with large boulders that could be used to his advantage. Kit's thoughts ticked over like a steam engine. One thing he knew for sure was that if someone ducked into water to elude someone else, at some point that person was going to have to leave the water. Every tracker kept an eye to the bank to discover at just what point that happened. And Kit was certain the Flatheads understood this too. All he had to do was to make them think he and Gray Feather had left the stream at some point where they did not. But there was a catch. A good tracker would anticipate this trick too.

A thin thread of crimson tinted the swift current. The cold water invigorated Gray Feather a bit, but he was beginning to stumble. The rush of water masked any sounds of pursuit, but just the same, Kit knew the Flatheads could not be far behind them.

He came to a wide, flat stone tilting out of the water. Leaving Gray Feather a moment, Kit climbed up it, leaving clear moccasin prints on its gray face. At the top he turned back and leaped into the stream again, taking up the slumping Ute and urging him on. If nothing else, the false trail would slow the following Flatheads until they discovered the trail went nowhere.

Another few dozen yards ahead, a low branch caught Kit's eye. This was what he had been looking for. After moving Gray Feather onto the rocky bank, Kit waded back out, leaped, caught the branch in both fists, and swung back and forth, abrading the bark with his fingers. Then, hand over hand, monkeylike, he scrambled to the bank, dropped, and made some prints in the grass along the coursing waterway. Finally he jumped through a bramble of wild raspberries, leaving an obvious trail of snapped twigs, and immediately scampered up another tree that brought him once again over the stream. For a second time he leaped back into the icy water, helped Gray Feather up, and carried the half-conscious man downstream a few dozen feet to a large boulder that stood away from the shore just far enough for the two men to squeeze behind.

"You think this is going to throw them off?" Gray Feather managed to say, struggling to remain conscious. Kit still had no idea how badly the Indian was wounded, but one thing was certain: He'd already lost a lot of blood.

"Just hang on thar, pard," he whispered, "and

keep low in the water. I'll get us out of here soon.''

Kit strained to hear above the rush of water but couldn't. Drawing the knife, he moved carefully out of cover with only his head showing above the water. He sidled around the boulder until he could just barely see past its rough edge. Up the stream a ways was the branch that he'd used to lay down his second false trail. He figured that the Flatheads would have been expecting such a ploy the first time, but having already given them one red herring to follow, he hoped that they would take this second one more seriously.

Suddenly he saw movement along the far bank. Three Flatheads were stalking through the brush there, the rushing water muffling the sound of their advance. Not far behind them, a party of Flatheads was wading in the water, looking for signs. Two Bulls was at its head.

Two Bulls came to the overhanging branch and stopped. He stared up at it, read the sign that Kit had purposefully left behind, and immediately ordered two braves to follow the trail that led up onto the bank. These two were joined by the three already on dry ground, and between them they fanned out. One shouted when he discovered the bramble Kit had run through. They powwowed a minute and then set off to run down the false lead.

But it took only a few minutes before the braves returned, disappointed, and informed Two Bulls that the trail had played out like the last one.

''This white man is a clever one,'' Two Bulls said, staring downstream. ''But I am beginning to know how he thinks.'' He gave a signal, and the war party pressed on.

Kit stepped back behind the boulder and lowered himself into the stream until only his nose and eyes showed above the water. He could hear the splashing of the Flatheads' advance, and when he had calculated that they were almost at the other side of the boulder, he prepared to sink beneath it.

But just then Kit spied the thin tendrils of red swirling out on the current. Gray Feather's blood would be a clear marker, pointing a finger directly at them. If the crimson flow should be spotted . . . Before Kit could ponder the results of such an unlucky accident, Two Bulls appeared past the edge of the boulder.

"Hold your breath," Kit whispered in Gray Feather's ear, and, clutching the Ute's buckskin shirt, sank below the water, dragging his friend down with him.

Although he was competent enough at keeping himself from drowning, swimming had never played a big part in Kit's life, and consequently he had never practiced the fine art of holding his breath for more than just a few seconds at a stretch. And he had no idea how well Gray Feather could manage the task either. Since he was wounded, and nearing unconsciousness, Kit figured the Indian would be no better at it than he, and maybe even a little worse. Once below the rushing waters, he had no way of following Two Bulls's progress. For all he knew, the Flathead warrior had spotted the blood sign and was even now following it back to its source. At this very moment Two Bulls might be standing three feet from him, probing the depths with the point of his war lance— and Kit would not know it until the point found him or Gray Feather.

The thought was not comforting, and neither was

the burning pressure he had begun to feel deep in his chest. His lungs began to cry out for air, but Kit resisted the urge. Gray Feather began to struggle against his grip. *Just five seconds longer,* he told himself, and when the time had elapsed, he demanded just five seconds more.

Gray Feather was struggling harder now. Even though Kit knew that they needed to remain hidden longer, it was becoming increasingly difficult for him to resist the compelling urge to explode to the surface and gulp in the life-giving air that their bodies so desperately demanded. When finally he could not remain submerged one second longer, and Gray Feather had become more than a handful to keep down, Kit straightened his knees and shot through the water's surface.

He dragged in a huge lungful of air, and at the same instant the knife in his fist leveled in front of him, ready to take on Two Bulls or the other Flathead warriors searching the water for them.

Chapter Six

Gasping up out of the water and knowing that he could be face-to-face with Two Bulls's war party, Kit figured that they were both gone beaver.

As the water streamed off his hair and out of his eyes, however, he was amazed to discover that the fierce warrior was not standing immediately over them with war lance poised high for the killing blow. Two Bulls and the others were nowhere to be seen. Drawing in another ragged breath, Kit suspected that the warriors might still be right around the boulder and about to strike. The sound of Gray Feather and him gasping for air would certainly have drawn their attention!

Kit glanced in a dozen different directions in those first few seconds, trying to determine the direction of the attack. But no attack came. As the sound of the water dripping off them mingled with the steady rush of the fast stream, Kit realized that the pursuers had indeed passed them by and were even now almost a hundred feet down the swift waterway.

He could hardly believe their good fortune. "I think we gave them the slip, Gray Feather," he whispered with a note of sheer amazement in his voice. "They went right on past us and never knew at all!"

The Ute did not reply.

Kit lifted the nearly unconscious man into his arms and struggled up the rocky bank. Casting a final glance down the stream where the Flatheads had disappeared, he carried Gray Feather into the forest, keeping to hard ground where his trace would be hardest to follow if Two Bulls should decide to backtrack on them.

"Where are we?"

Gray Feather's question brought Kit's head around. For the last hour Kit had been hunkered down on a ledge of rock, surveying the forest below. But so far there was no sign of Two Bulls's warriors. Ducking his head under a low rock shelf, Kit crab-walked back into the small cave he had discovered and in which he had laid out his unconscious partner. A small fire crackled in the tight confines, lending a bit of flickering light and some heat to the damp place.

"I was wondering when you were going to wake up, Gray Feather."

The Ute glanced around, then at Kit. "A cave?"

"Not much of one, but enough to get you and me out of sight until you heal up some."

Gray Feather's hand moved to the strip of deerskin covering the wound at his side.

"The bullet cut clean through your bacon and

missed your gut by a cat's whisker," Kit told him. "I'd say you're one lucky Injun. But that jog we took to shake Two Bulls and his boys spilled a lot of blood." Kit frowned. "I managed to stop the bleeding, then I packed it with some moss. It ain't much of a doctorin' job, I'm sorry to say, but it's the best I can do with nothing but a knife and some hide. Looks like you and me are gonna be holed up here for a few days until you get your strength back."

Gray Feather licked his lips. "I'm thirsty."

"Not surprised, considering all that blood you left behind. Got nothing to carry water in, but now that you're awake, I'll go fix up something. At least I still have Man With Many Horses's knife." Kit shoved the blade under his belt. "I'll try to snare us a rabbit or coon for food, too."

He left the wounded man there, taking a steep trail back into the forest. Finding a grove of aspen trees, Kit fashioned a crude bowl from a sheet of bark to carry water in. On his way to a little stream, he happened to spot a rabbit. He spent about ten minutes chasing after it and flinging rocks like an addlepated fool. But that proved as useless as shoveling hay into the wind. Frustrated and winded, Kit contrived a snare and set it in a trail that appeared to be heavily traveled and that led down to a pool of water.

Returning to the cave as night began to stretch out over the mountains, Kit helped Gray Feather drink some water, then added more wood to the fire to drive off the chill. He doctored Gray Feather with fresh moss he had gathered, then settled down at the mouth of the cave to watch the stars come out from behind the high, drifting clouds.

"Sorry to be holding you up, Kit," Gray Feather

said after a while. "I'll be fit for travel in a day or two, then we can be out of here."

"Whal, it ain't exactly like you went and got yourself shot on purpose," Kit replied, staring to the east where a faint glow brightened the night sky—probably Calling Elk's village, Kit judged.

Gray Feather was silent for a few moments, then said, "I can hardly believe it. Why would anyone want to break apart beaver dams and kill game for no reason . . . and murder the Flatheads? What could anyone have against them that would make them do that?"

Kit had been pondering those very same questions since making good their escape from Two Bulls's war party. As he ruminated over the problem now, he scanned the dark forest from their high vantage point, looking for something that he knew had to be out there.

"It doesn't make a lick of sense to me either, Gray Feather. And I ain't completely convinced it's happening like Calling Elk says."

"You saw those two men Smythe brought in. And Man With Many Horses said that they had recovered rifles. American rifles, not British."

Kit glanced over at the wounded man. Gray Feather was sitting up against the back of the shallow cave where flickering firelight played softly over his haggard face and naked chest. Kit had cut Gray Feather's shirt to make a wide bandage to hold the moss in place atop his wound. What remained of the shirt now served as a pillow against the cold rock.

"British. It keeps coming back around to that, don't it?" Kit went on.

"Well, they don't use any of the John Russell's

Green River Works knives, at least not as far as I
know.''

"No, but thar knives do carry a 'G.R.' up by the
hilt.'' Kit examined the example he'd taken from Man
With Many Horses. It was typical of the trade knives
being supplied to the Indians by the Hudson's Bay
Company. A good, solid Sheffield knife. The "G.R."
stamped on it, however, did not stand for Green
River, but for George Rex. The difference was obvious, and hardly anything Calling Elk would be con-
fused over.

"Did you manage to get a look at the knife Smythe
showed Calling Elk, Kit?''

"No, how about you?''

"It was too far.''

"Whal, ol' Calling Elk wasn't born yesterday. If it
was a Green River what scalped them two bucks,
reckon he'd know one to see one. A Green River's
plenty different from one of these British scalpers.
And he's handled plenty of English trade goods, from
what I seen of his camp.'' As he spoke, Kit continued
to gaze out across the dark forest below. He did not
recognize any prominent landmark, but he was certain
now that the glow against the dark sky *was* Calling
Elk's village. Yet he still hadn't spied what he suspected lay out there somewhere.

"I think Bridger would be anxious to know what's
going on up here, don't you, Kit?''

"Since it's his boys being accused of the mischief,
I reckon ol' Gabe would be right curious to get to the
bottom of this . . . and so would I.''

"As soon as I'm able to travel, we'll go back and
tell him.''

Kit looked at his partner again. "Back?''

"Well, yes. We *are* going back, now, aren't we? After all, we have no guns and you've only got that one knife. Anyway, the message we were carrying to Major Collins is gone too." Gray Feather stopped with the creases of a sudden scowl digging into his forehead. "I'm not sure I like the look I'm seeing on your face, Kit."

"Bridger gave us a job to do, and so far we ain't done it."

"Yes, but—"

"King George's boys have made some powerful claims against some of our boys, and I figure it's time we get down to the bottom of it."

"We?"

"Whal, me, seeing as you're not fit to travel."

"Alone?"

Kit nodded.

"What do you have in mind?"

"Seems to me that every which way I study out this problem, the compass needle keeps swinging around and settling on one point."

"And what's that?"

"The British."

Gray Feather grimaced. "It does seem that they have taken more than just a passing interest in the matter."

"Since you ain't going to do much traveling for the next few days, I was thinking that I'd just take a stroll on over to their camp and ask Mr. Alexander Smythe a few questions."

"He didn't appear to be a sociable sort of gent, Kit."

"Oh, I think I can make him come around." Kit

glanced at the knife in his hand, then slipped it back under his belt and stood up.

"You're going to talk to him right now?"

"Nope. I reckon right now I'll go and get us our belongings back, and that letter that Gabe entrusted to me to take to the Major."

"You're going back to the village?" Gray Feather asked, alarm suddenly in his voice.

"Sitting up here and waiting for you to heal ain't going to get the job done." Now that Kit was up on his feet, his angle of view had shifted, and there, in the vastness of the black forest below, was what he had been searching for. His lips twitched into a tight grin as he glanced back at Gray Feather. "It'll probably be late before I get back. I'll see what I can do about fetching you something to eat."

Fixing the location of the distant campfire, then shifting to the soft sky-glow of Calling Elk's village, Kit firmly established each position in his brain. Satisfied that he could find them both again, he took the shadowy trail down to the forest floor and melted silently into its deep gloom like a ghost.

Alexander Smythe strode out of the dark forest toward the blazing campfire where the men in his fur brigade sat working on various projects—some cleaning rifles, others repairing traps, one stitching new moccasins, another making diary entries, and at least one of the men reading by the firelight. The stomp and thump of Smythe's heavy footsteps ceased all at once. He had paused to scowled at the three crates stacked at the edge of camp. The tarp he had ordered them covered with was still folded and sitting atop the wooden boxes.

"Mr. Port!" Smythe's strident voice shattered the peaceful camaraderie of the camp. By the fire, Wilber Port's head came up with a snap and all about him the conversations fell into dead silence.

"Er . . . yes, Capt'n?" Port swallowed hard as the gaze of the men in camp fell upon him. Some of the eyes held pity, while others glistened in anticipation of a bit of excitement.

Smythe stood a moment glaring, then slowly dragged the shortened saber from its sheath and tapped the top crate. "I believe I had asked you to cover these boxes, Mr. Port," he said with a sudden chilling calm that would make a dead man's bones shiver—the calm that generally preceded the storm, perhaps?

Port immediately set down the rifle he had been cleaning and stood. "It must have slipped my mind," he confessed nervously. "I'll see to it now."

"Please do." Smythe's unnatural cordiality resonated through the camp like a fiddle string plucked by a bungling amateur.

Port hurried over to the crates and unfolded the tarp. "I got busy helpin' Warrington with the horses, Capt'n." He grinned sheepishly. "I'd have got to it later."

"Warrington, huh? Is Warrington captain of this fur brigade?"

"Er, no—"

The short sword swung up suddenly, catching Port alongside the face with the flat of its blade. Port wheeled around and plowed into the ground. Smythe straddled the fallen man and placed the tip of the saber to his jugular. "I'm captain of this here brigade, understand, Mr. Port? Not Warrington or anyone else!"

The man on the ground nodded his head, his eyes riveted on the blade.

"When I give an order, I expect it to be carried out. Is that too much to ask of my men?"

Port's head instantly gave the proper response.

"You know, Mr. Port, I've had my eye on you of late. You've been falling down a bit. This morning you almost got me killed when you didn't put a bullet into that savage." Smythe fingered the black smudge on his cheek where the powder blast from Many Arrows's musket had seared the flesh. "What have you got to say for yourself?"

"I . . . I didn't mean to hesitate," he groveled. "It all happened so suddenly that it caught me off guard."

"Off guard?" Smythe rumbled, putting his peg onto Port's chest above his heart and transferring his weight to it. "The . . . next . . . time . . . you . . . bungle," Smythe growled, emphasizing each word with increasing pressure on Port's chest until the squirming man cried out in pain, "it will be *your* bloody scalp I'll be taking to Calling Elk. And he won't know it didn't come off a bloody Yank, like I'll tell him."

Sheathing his sword, Smythe removed the peg from Port's chest. "Now, get to covering those crates. Wouldn't want any of Chief Calling Elk's men to come visiting and get too curious about what's in them, now, would we?"

Port rubbed the painful place on his chest, glancing around at the men chuckling among themselves at his disgrace. His face reddened and a slow fire of hate began to smolder in his eyes, a fire burning hotter by the second, swiftly consuming him. As Smythe turned away, Port sat up and spied a four-foot length of tree limb near the fire. All at once, he grabbed it up and lurched to his feet.

"Bully me, will you, you one-eyed, one-legged bastard!" Port roared, swinging the thick cudgel at the brigade leader's head.

Smythe came around, ducking instinctively, as if knowing exactly what the man had in mind. In an instant his sword cleared its sheath, and as Port wheeled the club around for another try, Smythe easily parried the blow, stepping effortlessly under it. For all his bulk, and the handicap of having only one good leg and one good eye, Smythe moved with a flowing gracefulness that startled his enraged adversary. He used the peg to his advantage, pivoting upon it with more freedom than a whole foot could offer.

His blade snicked this way and that, keeping the heavy club at bay. It moved like lightning in his well-schooled grip, and for a moment Smythe seemed to be playing with Port as a cat might a wounded bird he'd just caught, tossing it and then pouncing.

Port managed at first to back away from the quick jabs, but his club, although having greater reach, was useless against Smythe's superior skill. The old mountain pirate laughed at Port's feeble attempts, and then with a sudden rush the brigade captain lunged low, stepping quickly forward, and drove the blade through the startled man's heart.

With a quick yank he withdrew the crimson blade. For a moment Port stood there shocked, his wide eyes staring at the long sliver of steel that had pierced his chest. He began to speak, then his eyes rolled up in his head and he collapsed.

Smythe wiped the blade upon the dead man's shirt, then wheeled toward the silent, staring men sitting around the campfire. "Marsten!"

Aston Marsten snapped out of his stupor. "Gov'nor?"

"Over here."

A reluctance born of good, common sense attempted to keep him anchored firmly to the ground, but Marsten fought against its pull, knowing the consequence of crossing this unpredictable man. If Smythe's reputation for ruthlessness had previously been forgotten, the truth of it had just been driven home to them again. Marsten stood and hesitantly approached the brigade leader.

"Wot . . . er, wot can I do for you, Gov'nor," he stammered, his eyes held by the corpse at his feet.

"Scalp him."

His gaze leaped toward the brigade leader. "G' blind me! Wot did you say?" Marsten exclaimed, startled.

"His scalp. I want it now!"

No man there would have dared cross Smythe at that moment. Swallowing down his disdain over the task given him, Marsten removed his butcher knife and, kneeling over his fallen comrade, did his boss's bidding.

"Warrington!" Smythe rasped.

The trapper leaped obediently to his feet and came over.

"Since it was because of you that Port didn't do his job, I'll just let you finish it," he said, rapping the crates with his saber.

"Right away."

As the mountain pirate strode away, Warrington

spread the tarp over the crates. He did an excellent job of it, the best he could, for he understood that anything less could leave a man of Alexander Smythe's fur brigade very dead!

Chapter Seven

Once his eyes adjusted to the blackness of the forest, Kit was able to cut swiftly through the dark timber, moving with the same ease and confidence that another man, born to city life, might exhibit strolling along a city sidewalk at midday. It wasn't long before Kit caught a glimpse of firelight flickering through the black trees somewhere ahead in the endless darkness. He slowed his pace and cautiously eased behind the trunk of an ancient ponderosa pine at the edge of the forest. Chief Calling Elk's camp sat across the grassy plain. Fires burned in three or four locations, casting their dancing crimson reflections against the lodges there.

Kit settled down to wait.

It would still be hours before the camp was asleep, and that left Kit with time to ponder a few things that had bothered him since the beginning. He considered

73

all that the Flatheads were accusing the Americans of doing. Kit knew of a couple of trappers who in the past had shot game on a whim, just to see who was the better marksman, or whose rifle packed the biggest wallop. But that was rare. Ball and powder were too valuable to waste on such frivolous sport! And he'd known some men to sample the camp peddler's whiskey a little too freely and go sort of wild and bust up another man's camp. But that usually happened only during the rendezvous, where men generally expected and tolerated such behavior and no one paid it much mind—except perhaps the fellow whose lodge was ripped down. And as far as Kit could remember, he'd never heard of any trappers purposely breaching a beaver dam. Beaver was their livelihood. What kind of man would do that ... and why?

And murdering Indians? That happened sometimes. Usually in self-defense, or to punish bands of horse thieves. Certainly no American would murder a friendly Flathead just to stir up a hornet's nest. There were already plenty of tribes in these mountains eager to lift a white man's scalp. Why go out of your way to increase their numbers?

Kit couldn't figure it out.

His thoughts kept coming back to that same puzzling question. Why?

The more he thought about it, the more Kit had a feeling that the trapper Smythe was somehow connected with the mystery.

But then it revolved back to that same question again.

No matter how Kit turned the dilemma over in his brain, the *why* of it was not there.

The mountain air grew chilly as he waited, watching the moon creep lower in the sky and the campfires across the way fade and wink out one by one. The long wait gave Kit time to reflect on other things.

His thoughts drifted from the problem at hand back to a time when problems were largely unknown. Back to his childhood, and his father. Lindsey Carson had died when Kit was but nine years old, but still the memory of him remained razor sharp. Now, as he huddled in the dark shivering from the mountain chill, he suddenly thought of the sultry nights back in Missouri. The Flathead encampment momentarily wavered before his mind's eye, and in its place stood the long, cleared fields of their farm with their straight rows of corn standing tall and gray beneath a full Missouri moon—to a nine-year-old, everything seemed tall, especially his father.

He recalled Lindsey sitting next to him on the dark porch of their two-story cabin, heavy boots propped upon the top rail, chair canted back, face softly illuminated by the red glow of the tobacco in the pipe he always smoked in the evening after the day's chores were finished.

At times like this Lindsey usually had a tale or two to tell about the days when he and his brothers fought the Creeks and the Cherokees, and the British during the Revolutionary War and, later, in the War of 1812. Kit would listen for hours, vicariously living his father's adventures as if it had been he who had wielded the rifle and bayonet. And somehow, when the story was finished, there would be a hollow, longing feeling within him. He had missed out on something important—he seemed to have known that intuitively, even though he was still a tyke. The Carsons had been warriors and adventurers clear back to Scotland, where the clan originated. Sometimes Kit would lie awake at night, in the loft among his sleeping brothers, wondering if the world he had been born into had become too civilized, a place where warriors and adventurers might soon not be needed.

The night had grown colder, and a violent shiver shook him from his reverie. Memories of his past faded, replaced with the here and now, and the dark Flathead encampment across the way. A thin smile creased Kit's face as he realized that he hadn't missed any of the adventure after all. He'd just done what Carsons had always done: moved west and found the adventure that lay there waiting for them.

Kit stretched and flexed his fingers against the cold that had penetrated his buckskin britches and hunting shirt. His keen eyes took in the camp and noted that only a single fire flickered somewhere among the lodges. He saw no one moving, but that meant nothing. Kit knew there would be at least one sentry strolling among the sleeping lodges . . . maybe more, and probably a dog or two with them. Not that these Flatheads had suspected any trouble tonight. Posting guards at night was just the way people survived when they lived in a wilderness.

Kit didn't immediately spy the sentry, so he waited. A few minutes later a dark form passed by the lone fire. Once Kit spotted the man it was easy to follow his course, mapping it in his brain until he knew the circuit that would surely be followed over and over again throughout the night. Easing out of cover, he sprinted across the dark ground and dropped quietly behind one of the outer lodges.

. Clutching the knife that he had taken from Man

With Many Horses, Kit slipped silently into the village. He had calculated his approach so that the guard would be at the far edge of the village about now. Without wasting a moment more than necessary to assure himself the way was clear, Kit dashed low across the dark ground, settling noiselessly behind the lodge belonging to Calling Elk.

Man With Many Horses had told them that Calling Elk usually retained all weapons that were brought into his village. It was only logical to believe that his and Gray Feather's rifles and hunting bags—and Bridger's dispatch—were within Calling Elk's lodge now.

Kit grimaced to think about it. This was not something that he relished doing. He'd snuck into Indian camps before, generally to retrieve stolen horses. But the thought of creeping into a dark lodge among its sleeping inhabitants sent a shiver up his spine that had nothing to do with the cool night air.

Taking a long, settling breath, Kit lifted the edge of the door flap a fraction of an inch and peeked inside. It took a moment for his eyes to adjust to the deeper darkness within the lodge. When they had, Kit was able to see Calling Elk on one side, his wife on the far side, and a child of ten or eleven curled up against the back of the lodge. The soft, even breathing was reassuring. It told Kit that everyone was asleep, and since the interior remained blessedly quiet, Kit knew that there was no dog inside either. A dog would have made his quest entirely impossible unless he could kill it quickly and silently.

Kit suddenly pulled back into the shadows.

The sentry had started back across the center of village and had paused to peer up at the starry sky.

77

He held his musket casually by the barrel over his left shoulder. As Kit watched, the guard shifted the London Fusil to his right shoulder, yawned, stretched hugely, and started off in another direction.

Kit let go of a long breath. He hadn't a moment to lose. Without hesitating, he raised the door flap and poked a leg silently inside. In an instant he was within Calling Elk's lodge, where he froze, hardly breathing.

No one stirred.

Calling Elk's wife began to snore softly on her side of the lodge while the chief's even breathing continued uninterrupted from his side. As he hunkered there, guarding the sound of his own breathing, Kit looked around the small dwelling, noting where everything had been placed so that he'd not accidentally upset an item and bring the camp down on him. But mainly he was searching for the rifles.

He spotted them near one wall about eighteen inches from Calling Elk's right shoulder.

The floor was covered with bearskins that muffled the infinitely slow progress Kit made as he crept toward the rifles. His heart thumped so loudly, he feared the sound of it might give him away. But still the three people slept on. With great patience, Kit reached across the sleeping chief for the first rifle, gripped the barrel, and dragged it slowly—oh, so slowly—into his arms. Sweat beaded upon his brow in spite of the chill in the air. He worked his way back to the door and, after checking first that the guard was somewhere else, deposited the piece outside.

Ten minutes later Kit set the second rifle outside, alongside the first. The task seemed endless, but now only the two hunting bags remained. Kit returned for them. By now he knew precisely where every item within the lodge lay. He'd also concluded that the chief and his family were mighty sound sleepers.

Perhaps because of that Kit became a bit too confident, or perhaps it was that Providence had allotted him just so much time to do what needed to be done . . . and not one minute more.

The bags were almost beyond his reach, up near Calling Elk's head. Kit stretched an arm across the sleeping chief, groped, caught the strap in his fingertips, and, balancing awkwardly on knees and one hand, lifted it up, over, and—

The hunting bag slipped. Kit froze as it plopped soundly upon the bearskin blanket covering Chief Calling Elk's chest.

Calling Elk's eyes snapped open with a start, but before he could determine what had awakened him, Kit's hand came down over his mouth and the knife pressed hard against the chief's jugular. Both men's eyes fastened upon each other, and Kit whispered near his ear, "You make a sound and it will be your last." Then, fearing the chief might disregard his own safety in this matter, Kit added, "And then your wife and son will be next."

That gave the Flathead leader something to think about.

"You understand my words?"

Calling Elk nodded his head, his wide, dark eyes fixed upon Kit.

Kit's thoughts raced ahead. One sound from this man could bring a dozen warriors down on him in moments. He had to find a way to ensure the chief's silence and yet give himself time enough to escape the village. He could cut the man's throat. No one would know until morning. But that wasn't Kit's way.

And if he did, there would be no way to avert a war between the Americans and Flatheads. A war was the last thing Kit wanted to start. If anything, he was bound to try to prevent one if he possibly could . . . if he ever made it out of here with his hair in place.

He considered his choices. Not that he had very many, or that he had any time to ponder them thoroughly. He could see only one way out, and that was to somehow take the chief with him, to do it quietly enough not to arouse his sleeping wife and son, and to get him out of the village without the sentry seeing them.

That was all.

Kit grimaced as these thoughts flashed through his brain, and he came to a decision at once. His father had more than once told Kit that he was an impulsive soul, and that someday it would get him in trouble. But so far Kit had been able to wheedle himself out of any predicament his rashness had gotten him into. Maybe this time his haste would be his undoing, but the decision had been made. Cautiously he eased the pressure on Calling Elk's mouth. The chief made no sound, his eyes slanted down as far as they could go, staring at the dull blade resting firmly on his throat.

"You're coming with me. If you don't make a sound, you will live. If you do, you're a gone beaver. Know what that means?"

Calling Elk's wide riveting look told him he didn't.

"It means you're gonna be a dead Injun if you don't do exactly what I tell you to do."

The woman across the way coughed and tossed in her sleep. Kit stiffened, applying more pressure to the blade against the chief's throat as a warning. She rolled in her blanket, then rolled again, and in another moment her breathing evened out and the soft purring snore resumed.

"Understand now?" Kit whispered sharply.

Calling Elk managed a slight, almost imperceptible nod of his head.

Kit slipped the hunting bags over his shoulder and hurriedly fumbled out of one a folded piece of cotton ticking that he used to cut patches from. He shoved this into the chief's mouth and bound it in place with a rawhide thong.

Kit inclined his head at the doorway. "One sound, and I'll be sending you on your way to the land of your ancestors. Got that?"

Calling Elk merely glared at him as he lifted back the covers, grabbed up his moccasins and a shirt, and soundlessly slipped out the door. Outside, Kit breathed a huge sigh. He was halfway there. The guard was on the far side of the village. Fortune hadn't completely abandoned him yet. Kit took up the rifles and poked one of them into Calling Elk's spine. The chief moved off without making a sound, and five minutes later both men were deep in the forest, heading back toward the cave. It was only then that Kit felt the strain of the last few hours.

Few hours?

Kit was shocked to see the sky already beginning to brighten to the east. The job had taken all night, and he had hardly realized it. At least he had gotten their rifles back. He'd left behind a brace of pistols and their tomahawks, but that couldn't be helped now.

"You can remove the gag, Chief," Kit said once they were far from the village.

Calling Elk untied the thong, spit out the ticking,

and glared over his shoulder. "Many warriors will follow."

"I'm sure they will. Reckon you and me will just have to leave no tracks." Kit knew he'd have to watch the chief closely to make certain the crafty fellow didn't lay down a trail for his warriors to follow.

"Where are you taking me?"

"Someplace safe for a while until I can think this thing through. I'd have left you sleeping in your lodge if things went the way I'd planned them. I didn't want to take you, but this was the only way to keep you quiet long enough for me to get away."

They walked along a moment longer before Chief Calling Elk stopped and turned back to face Kit. His dark eyes narrowed suspiciously. "You could have cut my throat and fled like the fox with no one knowing."

"Yep, I could have done that, Chief. The notion did cross my mind. But you see, that just ain't my way. It ain't *our* way . . . in spite of what you might have been told about us bloodthirsty Americans."

When the next morning came and the tribe discovered their chief missing, no one thought too much about it at first. Commonly, folks arose early and went off to meditate on life or the world around them, so Calling Elk's disappearance was not such an odd thing. Everyone expected him to return shortly. No one even considered that their chief had been kidnapped until his wife emerged from her lodge wearing a puzzled and vaguely concerned look.

"What is troubling you, Singing Wind?" one of the women of the village asked.

"My husband left our lodge early." Her forehead

wrinkled in a sudden, pinched scowl. "It is not like him."

The other woman laughed softly. "It is the way of men sometimes."

"Yes, but the strange thing is that he took with him the weapons which belonged to the white men who fled yesterday. This is not his way."

Her friend agreed that it was strange behavior, and when word of it finally spread through the village some of the men strolled over to investigate the matter further. One of them spotted some unusual tracks beside the lodge, and a few minutes later they discovered the trail of an intruder: where he had entered the village, where he had remained waiting beside the chief's lodge, and where he and Calling Elk had left the village later.

The alarm was sounded, and before the hour was up Two Bulls had organized a party of men to go after their chief. Man With Many Horses joined them in spite of the burning stares of hate that his chief rival gave him.

Two Bulls was not alone in his disapproval of this "interloper." Although Man With Many Horses was generally liked by the Flatheads, many men yet distrusted him—particularly Hump and Stalking Wolf. Both were close friends of Two Bulls. Stalking Wolf was a first cousin of Mary Fawn Hiding. He had been almost as upset about his cousin marrying an outsider as Two Bulls had been, and the event only served to bind the two men, and Hump, closer in a triangle of hatred toward the Ute who had come to live in their midst.

Hump was a huge warrior with a lumpy, round face and shoulders like a buffalo's—hence his name.

Stalking Wolf, on the other hand, could almost be called delicate. He was a small man with a finely sculpted face and eyes that constantly darted about as if always on the lookout for some danger . . . or deviltry. Eyes that never stopped long enough to look a person square in the face.

The three were fitting company for each other, and as they started off on the trail of their kidnapped chief, they exchanged glances that, if Man With Many Horses had seen them, might have made him reconsider going off with them on this hunt.

Chapter Eight

Smythe strolled through the sleeping camp as a captain might prowl the decks of his ship: a keen eye to the riggings and sails, a glance at the helmsman, who in this case was a man named Carter Brown, manning his post as third-shift night guard.

Brown gave Smythe a wave indicating that all was quiet and secure.

Smythe glanced at the skyline to the east where a faint rosy glow marked the coming of dawn. To the west the high ground was just beginning to emerge from the darker forest surrounding it. It was that point of high ground that Smythe intended to explore this morning. The season of prime pelts was long past, and soon he'd be leading his fur brigade back to Fort Vancouver for the remainder of the summer. But come fall they'd all head out again. This Flathead country had proven to be fine beaver country for the

Hudson's Bay Company, and Smythe intended to return. He judged that the higher ground to the west might hold promise, and he wanted to take a look before leaving. He needed to discover more rich beaver ground, since he and his men had nearly trapped this area clean.

And it should remain that way for some time, considering the havoc I've wrecked on the beaver dams.

A slash of a grin cut his bearded face. That in itself should discourage the Americans! Instinctively his fingers went to the patch over his left eye and the hatred within him burned. If they insisted on invading his personal trapping grounds, the Flatheads were going to have something to say about it. Smythe was making sure of that!

With his peg leg Smythe kicked a foot sticking out from beneath a blanket.

"Wot?" Marsten mumbled groggily.

"Get up. You're coming with me."

He levered himself up onto his elbows and scrubbed the sleep from his eyes. "With you? Wot time is it?"

"Get dressed. There's some coffee on the fire. You and me are going to take a look at that ridge across the way."

Marsten groaned, but he crawled out of his blankets just the same and stood, stretching and working the kinks out of his back. Sleeping on cold, hard ground took its toll on men—some sooner than others, but always in the end it was the ground that won out.

Smythe and Marsten rode away from the campsite with the morning sun still below the mountain peaks, but the sky was already bright. The high ridge of land to the west shone in a brilliant yellow glow—a pool of molten gold upon the dark blanket of forest still sleeping in night's shadows.

"Wot are you expectin' to find over there, Gov'nor?"

Smythe shot a narrow glance of impatience at the smaller man. "Beaver," the captain replied with an edge of irritation. "What else?"

Marsten winced and knew better than to cross this man—this pirate with the powder-keg temper. He adjusted the long rifle in the crook of his arm and said, "You figuring on pulling out of here soon?"

"Soon," Smythe answered brusquely.

"Wot about the Americans?"

"I've built a fire under Calling Elk. He'll make it plenty hot for any American who comes on through looking for beaver."

Marsten chuckled. "I wouldn't want to be one of 'em. Say, what do you suppose ever happened to them Yanks wot managed to escape the old chief, anyway?"

"They're fifty miles away by now if they have an ounce of sense about them," Smythe said, and gave a short, rumbling laugh. "You got to hand it to them bloody Yanks, though, getting clean away like they did. Calling Elk's boys were burning up with revenge when we brought those two Flatheads in across their ponies and blamed their murder on the Americans." Smythe's hand went to his face, his rough finger stroking the black cloth of the patch there. "If I had my way I'd scalp every last one of them Yanks."

"You ain't got no love for them Americans, do you, Gov'nor?"

"They did this to me!" Smythe exploded, tearing off the patch, revealing the sunken hole where an eye

87

had once resided. "And this!" He lifted his peg from the leather pocket that served in place of a regular stirrup. "Love? I'd sooner love the devil and all his hordes than a single American!"

Marsten grinned at the venom in the brigade captain's voice. Smythe might be a ruthless and dangerous man to work for, but at least he kept life exciting.

The sky brightened, bringing color to the treetops. They rode with little talk. Smythe was not the sort of man you spoke to unless necessary. The land tilted toward the edge of a ravine, and as the two men drew near to it, Smythe suddenly reined to a halt and cocked his head, listening to some sound yet too faint for Marsten's ears.

Marsten cast a questioning look at the captain.

Smythe swung out of the saddle and, holding his reins, approached the edge of the ravine with caution. Marsten followed, mimicking the leader's wariness. They tied off their animals and went the final two dozen feet on their bellies.

"Wot is it?" Marsten whispered when he had elbowed his way up beside the big man.

Smythe's single eye scanned the wooded hillside that dropped to the bottom of the ravine, where a swift stream tumbled down the mountainside in its rocky channel. He studied the land for a moment, then pointed.

"Over there."

Marsten squinted, then his eyes widened in surprise. "G' blind me! That's Calling Elk!"

"It is," Smythe said with just a hint of surprise in his low voice.

"But who's the fellow behind the chief poking that rifle into his spine?"

88

Smythe scratched the shaggy beard encircling his face. "I've seen him before," he said wonderingly.

"Why, it's that same bloke wot was in Calling Elk's village when we brought them dead men back to his camp. The American wot got away!"

Smythe glanced at Marsten. "I believe you just might be right."

"But wot's he doing herding ol' Calling Elk that way? I thought you said he'd be fifty miles from here by now!"

"I said he would be if he had an ounce of sense," Smythe reminded him. "Apparently that fellow ain't too smart."

"Wot should we do about it? I can plug that Yank from here with no problem." Marsten shouldered his rifle and squinted down its long barrel.

Smythe pushed the barrel aside and shook his head. He pulled back from the edge of the ravine and sat up to think it over.

"You're going to kill the Yank, ain't you, Gov'nor?"

"Shut up and let me think!" Smythe's broad forehead wrinkled, and his one good eye narrowed. "If we kill the Yank and the chief, we can claim the two killed each other."

"Yeah, yeah," Marsten agreed eagerly, turning back to his rifle.

"Wait."

Marsten frowned impatiently.

"Someone's going to get suspicious if it's always me bringing in the bodies."

"Naw. Savages don't think that way."

"Don't bet on it."

"Then let me shoot just the Yank," Marsten implored.

Smythe tugged at the knots in his beard as he thought. "But there were two of them that got away. Where's the second man?"

"Wot does it matter?"

"If maybe we were to follow them they might lead us to that second Yank. And if we was to nab the two of them together, and free the chief . . ." Smythe considered the possibilities a moment. "Now, that would be a real feather in our caps, Marsten. The Flatheads would have the Americans back to deal with as they see fit, and lifting a couple scalps might be just what they need to stir them up enough and hit the warpath." Smythe chuckled low.

"Mean I can't shoot 'em now?"

Smythe cast him a burning scowl. "No, you bloody well can't shoot him now," he growled. "Come on, let's keep that Yank in sight and see where he's taking the chief."

"You don't have to like it, Chief, just do it. This is a darn sight better than me having your throat cut back thar in your lodge," Kit advised Calling Elk when the man balked at crossing the swift stream. "I know what you're thinking. I can see it in your eyes. You're thinking that this might be a good time to make a break. That maybe I'll let down my guard while we're wading down this cold water. Whal, don't you bet on it, Calling Elk."

"Many warriors will come after you."

"Just get yourself into that stream like I told you and let me worry about that."

Calling Elk frowned and, seeing that he had no

choice at the moment, stepped into the icy water and started down the stream with Kit and the big buffalo gun at his back. A few hundred feet farther on, Kit steered the chief onto dry land, ran him around a rocky outcropping to confuse the trail, then led him over some granite boulders and on toward the cave where he had left Gray Feather the night before.

After laying down a few more false trails, Kit was finally near the place. He directed Calling Elk toward the stream where he had set his trap the previous evening. The snare was still empty. His stomach grumbled unhappily and his body cried out for sleep, but both items were going to have to wait a little while longer.

Just before noon, Kit started Calling Elk up the narrow mountain-goat trail to the cave. He could have gotten this far hours earlier if he'd taken a more direct route, but Kit wanted to be certain the Flatheads could not follow him, so he had spent a considerable time backtracking and putting out traces that eventually led nowhere.

Even before he reached the cave, the delicious odor of roasting meat reached his nose.

"Gray Feather," Kit called out while still a dozen feet from the cave.

"I'm still here," came the reply.

Kit motioned the chief into the cave, bent low, and stepped inside behind him. The gloom was somewhat dispelled by the small fire that Gray Feather had kept burning. The wounded Ute was leaning up against the back wall, holding a heavy branch. It would make a mighty useful club to ward off panthers, bear . . . or Flatheads, Kit mused.

Gray Feather eyed the chief suspiciously, the club

pounding his fist threateningly. Just a reminder that although he had been wounded, he was not yet helpless. His eyes flashed momentarily to Kit when the mountain man stepped in behind the chief.

"I figured I'd bring you some company, Gray Feather," Kit replied to the question clearly written on the Ute's face.

"That was thoughtful of you, but I wasn't lonely."

"Too late to take him back now."

"What went wrong?"

"I got careless," Kit explained. "It was either take him along or send him on to his happy hunting grounds." Kit passed Gray Feather's rifle and hunting bag across to him. "But I did manage to get these back. How you feeling?"

"I've felt better."

"Reckon that's a fact." Kit turned to Calling Elk. "Make yourself comfortable, Chief. You'll be staying here with us a few days."

The Flathead said nothing, but lowered himself to the cold rock floor and permitted Kit to check the leather thongs with which he had bound his hands. Finding them still secure, Kit tied off one end to a spire of rock and then lowered himself cross-legged in front of the fire. "Rabbit!" he said, turning the spit over the fire. "How did you manage it? I have a snare set by a game trail, but it was empty."

Gray Feather smiled smugly, as if the task were but a small thing, and said, "You sound surprised."

"Whal, you're not in much shape to go hunting."

He laughed softly, holding the wound in his side to keep it from hurting too much, and admitted the truth. "Actually, it came hopping in here on its own a few hours ago. I just flung this American shillelagh at it before it saw me. Skinned it out and cleaned it with a sharp rock. The rest was easy.''

"And here I was worrying about finding something for you to eat." Kit probed the hot meat with a finger. "It appears to be about done. Hungry?"

"Starved."

"How about you, Calling Elk?"

The chief glanced over but said nothing.

Kit cut the rabbit apart and passed the pieces around after temporarily freeing Calling Elk's hands. The chief accepted the food and ate it down to the bones, stripping them clean. Kit and Gray Feather attacked the meat with equal enthusiasm, and inside of fifteen minutes there was nothing left of the rabbit but a pile of bones. Kit collected them up and tossed them far out into the forest to discourage any bears, just in case they came visiting.

Kit tied Calling Elk's hands again, then slipped his hunting bag over his shoulder and grabbed up his rifle.

"Where are you going now?" Gray Feather asked.

"Thar's a camp full of redcoats not far from here to the east. I still haven't paid them a visit yet. I intend to hunt them up and get to the bottom of these tales they've been spreading."

"Right now? You look all done in, Kit. Why don't you rest up first?"

"No time for that just yet. Keep an eye on the chief here, and I'll try to be back soon as I can."

Kit ducked out of the low cave and hurried down the steep trail, disappearing once more into the forest.

Chapter Nine

The two runners came jogging back to the main party of warriors. They had been in advance of the others, running down the trails as various traces became apparent. And as happened on two previous attempts, these runners bore back the disappointing news that the trace they had thought to be genuine had in fact been another clever ruse. Before they spoke the words that no one wanted to hear, Man With Many Horses already knew the report. Everyone knew the report, for the anger and disgust was written all over the messengers' faces.

"The trail goes nowhere," a willow-thin warrior with sharp features and sinewy muscles reported, breathing heavily after his long run. There was no time to waste now on walking.

"It merely vanishes among the rocks. Like the other traces we have followed," the other scout put in, his growing concern making itself known in the urgent edge in his voice.

Sitting astride his pony, Two Bulls scowled, then slammed his clenched fist into the palm of his hand. "This white man has the cunning of brother fox in him. Two times now he has managed to evade us."

"There is yet hope," Man With Many Horses said.

They considered him with mixed feelings. Some liked the outsider, respected his strength and bravery, and his counsel, which had always proven wise. Others still mistrusted him. Two Bulls never had anything good to say about the man whose good looks and strong character had won the heart of the woman he had wanted, even as his rich stable of horses had caught the eye of her father, the ultimate decision maker in matters of the heart where a daughter was concerned.

Man With Many Horses swung off his pony and examined the trail they had been following. "Look, the trace is still clear here," he said. "He is laying down false ways. It is up to us to discern the truth from the lie. It might take much time, but the puzzle will eventually be solved."

"Hah! You think you have a clearer vision than Moose Lodge or Mountain Smoke?" Two Bulls railed, pointing at the two runners who had just returned empty-handed.

Man With Many Horses let the barb sail past. Small things did not bother him. Words, least of all. He grinned at Two Bulls and said confidently, "Unless the white man has grown wings like our brother the eagle, and has carried Calling Elk through the air, then surely the marks of their passing must still remain. It is only for us to have eyes to find them."

The men chuckled at Man With Many Horses's simple but wise retort, and that only deepened the color in Two Bulls's face.

"Hold your counsel, interloper," Two Bulls snapped back, hatred flaring in his dark eyes. "It was your counsel that brought us to this place!"

"How so?" a warrior named Night Thunder demanded. His voice was as his name suggested, and when he spoke, he commanded attention.

"If it had not been for this outsider's bad counsel when we first captured the Americans, we would have killed them at once, and our chief would not have been taken away."

This gave them something to consider. Seeing that he had made inroads against his rival, Two Bulls slogged on, reminding them that it was Man With Many Horses who later invited Kit and Gray Feather into his lodge. And it had been Man With Many Horses who had allowed them to escape.

"He says the white man called Carson grabbed his knife from him, but who here among us was watching? Our eyes were all saddened by the butchered bodies of our brothers brought in by our friend Smythe. All we have is this outsider's word that he was attacked and overpowered. Let's not forget that he is a friend to one of them. A kinsman! Would Man With Many Horses not feel greater loyalty toward a kinsman than to our people? Carson did not simply escape! He was let go!"

Their view narrowed upon the new man among them. Stalking Wolf, Mary Fawn Hiding's cousin, added his say in the matter. "I have heard it spoken that you cannot trust the Utes. They not only ride to the resting place of the sun to steal horses, but they even steal them from each other! There is no truth in any of them.''

Man With Many Horses's hand shot out with the speed of a striking snake and his fingers encircled Stalking Wolf's throat. The startled man's eyes bulged. Man With Many Horses lifted Stalking Wolf off his feet until he balanced on his toes, and when he spoke, his voice was low and menacing. ''I have stolen horses from no man. All that I have, I have earned honorably through cunning, through battle, and through trading. And I did not let the white man escape. I did not aid my friend Gray Feather, either. All this talk is not helping Calling Elk. As we stand here our chief is being taken farther away by a man who is as clever a tracker as any one of us. One who would be a worthy foe for any Ute! But one, perhaps, who is too much of a warrior for the timid Flatheads. Flatheads, I am learning, prefer to bicker among themselves.''

''Again Man With Many Horses gives true counsel,'' Mountain Thunder rumbled. ''While we stand here fighting against each other, the white man and the Ute are making good their escape, taking our chief with them. If we don't find them soon, they will cross into the lands of our enemies, the Blackfeet, and then we will have even more to concern us. I say stop this useless fighting and find the Americans while they are still within our grasp.''

As ever where Man With Many Horses was concerned, the band was deeply divided. But in the end Mountain Thunder's words brought the men back together—at least temporarily—and they resumed their task of following the broken trail as best they could.

* * *

"G' blind me, Gov'nor, they're holed up in a cave!"

"I can see that," Smythe retorted tautly. "I'm not blind, and they're not deaf, so keep your bloody voice down."

The two Englishmen had followed Kit and Calling Elk at a safe distance, but they had closed that distance considerably once Kit and the chief started up the steep track to the cave high up on the cliff. Smythe and Marsten had left their horses a few hundred yards back and hurried forward until they were hunkered down in the deep forest, just below the cliffs. So close were they now that Smythe clearly heard the white trapper call out.

"Gray Feather?"

"I'm still here."

"So," Smythe whispered, his lip hitching up at one corner, "the other one is inside too."

"They are boxed in there with no way out except past the muzzles of our rifles."

"Like bloody rats in a cage," Smythe said.

"We can give them Flatheads three bodies!" Marsten gushed eagerly.

"No! I already told you. We take them prisoners and free the chief. Let the bloody Flatheads finish the Americans. I've given them gun and powder, and reason enough to use them! This kidnapping might just be all that's needed to finally set loose the whole Flathead nation on the Americans. And all I have to do is stand back and watch, and pour a little oil here and there on the flames to keep the fire burning."

Smythe hitched his head back the way they had come. "We'll bring the horses up so they'll be handy. Then we'll make our way up to that cave."

They moved off silently, and fifteen minutes later had picketed the horses and were making a wide loop around the outcropping. It took some searching, but finally Smythe spied a steep trail up to the top. Clawing their way up through the thick growth, they made the top and hurried back until they were near the ledge. Careful that his wooden peg didn't smack the rocks, Smythe readied his rifle and led the way around to the mouth of the cave.

For several long minutes after Kit had left the cave on his mission to track down the Hudson's Bay trappers and learn more about the slaying of Flathead Indians and the destruction of the beaver ponds, Gray Feather and Calling Elk sat looking at each other in utter silence.

For Gray Feather, gregarious fellow that he was, silence was intolerable. And without something to keep his mind off the bullet hole in his side, the burning wound had begun to ache painfully. Since it did not appear as if the chief was in any mood to break the silence, Gray Feather took the first step.

"I'm sorry you got dragged into this, Calling Elk," he said in the chief's own tongue. Gray Feather understood the Flathead language better than he could speak it, and although his words were clumsy, the stoic warrior squatting near the fire understood clear enough.

Calling Elk peered darkly at the younger man, and for a moment Gray Feather despaired of stirring up even the smallest conversation. Then the chief said, "Your people and my people are not at war. Why do you keep me bound like an enemy, and why have you aligned yourself with the American?"

"If I remember right, your people were getting ready to lift our scalps. That's why you are tied up now. And as far as Kit Carson is concerned, he is my friend."

Calling Elk grunted. "One must learn to choose his friends carefully."

"I believe I have."

"For many years we have been the friend of the American trappers too. See where that friendship has brought us. Many of my warriors have been killed. The time for peace and friendship is gone and the season to make war is come."

"And that's another reason why I'm keeping you tied up, Calling Elk. I know the Americans well. I have lived in their great villages for many winters, and I can tell you this, what you claim they have done is not their way. They are fierce warriors, and make strong war medicine when they have to. But for the most part, the men who come west want only peace, and to be allowed to trap the beaver for the gold its skins fetch back east. And believe me, Calling Elk, they fetch mighty little gold once the trappers get through with their carousing and gambling during the season of the rendezvous.

"They do not want war any more than you. It makes no sense to stir up trouble in a place where they have to work. And as for breaking up beaver dams, well, that's just plain ridiculous. Beaver is their stock-in-trade, their livelihood! A warrior who owns many horses would not go out in his field and shoot them for the fun of it."

"Yet, it has happened. We see their mischief all around us."

Gray Feather frowned. He couldn't deny that something peculiar was going on here. "Yes, I saw it too. And that is why Kit has gone off to get to the bottom of this. If there is a renegade out there doing all these things, then he will find him."

Calling Elk considered this, his face carved in stone, revealing nothing of the thoughts in his head. He glanced at the crude bandage wrapped around Gray Feather's waist. "You have been wounded?"

"One of your braves managed to wing me. It isn't serious, but I lost a lot of blood. Only just got it to stop bleeding a few hours ago. Hurts bad, but I can put the pain out of my mind when I'm otherwise occupied."

The chief nodded his head knowingly. Gray Feather had the notion that the old warrior had stopped a bullet or two in his lifetime.

"Your manner of speech is strange. You line up words in a way I have never heard before."

Gray Feather grinned. "It comes from living in the white man's villages and going to the white man's schools."

"Yes, but even the white men I have known do not speak as you."

"Well, some do. But most of them live back east— er, in the waking place of the sun."

"Hmm. I see much of the white man in you."

"My father was white," Gray Feather admitted. "But I spent the first half of my life living with my mother's people. That is when Man With Many Horses—he wasn't called that back then—and I became friends."

The chief started to speak, but a faint sound outside cut his words short. His head snapped around and he stared at the cave's mouth. Gray Feather heard it, too, and reached for his rifle. The next moment, two men ducked under the low entrance.

"Touch that rifle and you're a dead Injun," one of the men barked, his deep voice rumbling in the small cave.

Gray Feather's hand lingered a moment near the rifle, but his eyes were fixed on the big bore of the buffalo gun pointed at his chest. Slowly he withdrew his hand.

The man who had spoken was glaring fiercely through one eye.

A second man was crouching low, his rifle sweeping from side to side. "There were three of 'em. Wot happened to the third?"

"Smythe," Calling Elk said.

"You all right, Chief?"

"Yes."

"Lucky we seen you when we did. Where's the other fellow who brought you?"

"He left here. I do not know where he went, or how long he will be away."

"Damn, let the bloke slip through our fingers, we did, Gov'nor."

It don't matter now, so long as the chief is safe. Who's this fellow? He looks Injun."

"I am Indian. Ute, to be exact," Gray Feather answered with acrid indignation. "And I'd appreciate it if you would point that rifle in some other direction, sir."

"G' blind me, Gov'nor! Did them words come out of *his* mouth?"

Smythe frowned. "Ute? What are you doing running around with the Americans?"

"They are my friends."

"I regret to hear that. Marsten. Fetch that rifle away from the Ute, then cut the chief loose.

Freed from his bonds, Calling Elk rubbed his wrists and crawled farther out of the line of fire.

"Should I kill this Injun for you, Chief?"

"No."

Smythe glanced at Calling Elk. "He might have killed you."

"I do not think so."

"Aw, let me plug the varmint," Marsten whined. "We don't need him for nothing. It's the American we wanted."

"Shut up."

"We will take Gray Feather back to my village," Calling Elk insisted.

Smythe chewed his lip irritably, but in the end agreed. "All right. But I want to know about the American. Where did he go, Injun?"

Gray Feather knew better than to alert this glaring man that Kit had in fact gone out to find *him.* "I don't know."

Smythe thrust the barrel of his rifle into Gray Feather's chest, knocking him violently back against the cave's hard wall. "You lie to me again, Injun, and this rifle might just accidentally go off, in spite of the chief's wishes."

Gray Feather put a hand against his chest and winced. Smythe's finger went for the trigger. "All right," Gray Feather said. "He's off hunting. He figured we'd be holed up here, seeing as I took a bullet while escaping Calling Elk's village the other day." Gray Feather hoped he had said it with enough conviction that Smythe would buy the story.

Smythe glared at him a long moment, thinking it

103

over, then glanced at Calling Elk. "It that the straight of it, Chief? Is that where the American went?"

Gray Feather held his breath. The chief had heard Kit's plans, and a word now would mean sure death. Calling Elk looked at him, a spark of uncertainty in his piercing eyes.

"It is as he says. The white man spoke of going hunting."

Gray Feather let go of a long breath. Well, in a way it was what Kit had said. *I intend to hunt them up and pay them a visit* . . . had been his exact words. Thankfully, the chief had chosen not to elaborate on what Kit had intended to go hunting for. But why had he covered for Kit?

Smythe raised the barrel of his rifle slowly, and Gray Feather saw that the man with him, Marsten, was sorely disappointed that his execution had been put off.

"Get up!"

Gray Feather pushed himself forward, gritting back the pain in his side as he crawled to the entrance. Outside he tried to straighten up. The best he could manage was a hunched-over posture. Something hard jabbed him in the spine.

"Get moving, Injun," Smythe ordered.

Holding his side, Gray Feather began the long, painful climb down to the forest floor.

Chapter Ten

Gray Feather felt himself slowing down, and he knew he couldn't afford that.

But he couldn't help it, either.

He had lost too much blood. His brain was whirling, and on top of that, the wound in his side had begun to bleed again. He tried to push everything out of his fogging brain and force it simply to concentrate on putting one foot in front of the other . . . one foot in front of the other . . . one . . .

He staggered and caught himself.

He had to keep moving, to keep one step ahead of the relentless pair of men astride horses behind him. When he slowed beyond what the one-eyed man wanted, Smythe would ride forward and prod him viciously with that wooden peg fixed to his stump of a leg.

At one point Calling Elk put an arm around Gray Feather to help him along.

"Leave him alone," Smythe barked. "If he can't make it under his own steam, we'll ride over him and leave his corpse to the crows."

"Let me plug him right now," Marsten implored.

"Shut up."

Gray Feather straightened up a little, renewing his resolve, a hand pressed to his side to stem the seepage of blood. His brain repeated, *One foot in front of the other . . . one foot in front of the other . . .*

"Hey, Gov'nor, you ever pull the legs off a daddy longlegs?"

Smythe shot a glance at the grinning man but did not reply.

"That Injun, he reminds me of it. When you pluck off that first leg the bugger don't hardly notice the difference. But as you keep pulling 'em off, he starts to stagger about, like the bloody thing spent all day in the pub. When he finally gets down to just two legs, he don't know which way to go. Starts walking himself in a bloody circle, he does." Marsten laughed. "Sorta like that Injun there. He'd be walking circles now if it weren't for you keeping him in line."

Calling Elk glanced back at the leering man, but Gray Feather could not tell what he was thinking. Gray Feather ignored Marsten's words. He had more important things to concentrate on.

One foot in front of the other . . .

Marsten said, "Then you pull off that next leg and he just pulls himself along, not knowing that he's come to the end of his rope and ought to lay down and die. Keeps crawling along, one leg and all, just pulling his little round body after it like nothing's wrong. Then you pull off that last leg, and you know wot, Gov'nor?''

''What?''

Marsten slapped his hands together. ''You smash the bloody bugger all to hell!'' He laughed. Calling Elk looked away. Smythe chuckled, chewed his lip, and turned his eye back to the trail.

All at once the brigade captain reined his horse to a stop.

''Wot's up, Gov'nor?''

Smythe cocked an ear. ''Somebody's coming.''

Marsten drew back the hammer of his rifle.

Gray Feather had taken three or four steps before realizing that everyone else had stopped with Smythe. He commanded his legs to come to a halt, swayed, and stabbed back a leg to catch himself an instant before tumbling over. He felt sick to his stomach as he steadied himself against the trunk of a tree.

There was some movement in the trees ahead.

Calling Elk peered hard at it, then hurried a couple steps forward as the men on horseback came into view. It was the Flatheads, with Two Bulls at the head.

''Calling Elk!'' Two Bulls exclaimed. ''We have found you, and you are unharmed.''

''The Americans did not hurt me.''

''Our people feared for your life.''

Calling Elk managed a small smile of appreciation.

''You escaped from them? Tell us how.''

''It was the trappers Smythe and Marsten who found me.''

Two Bulls looked at the Englishmen. ''Once again you have proven your friendship to our people.''

Smythe gave him a thin smile. Gray Feather had to

blink when he saw it, for to him it appeared more like a snarl. If it was so, however, the Flatheads seemed not to notice. "Your people and my people have been friends for a good number of winters, Two Bulls. And I'd like to keep it that way. Seems to me that we're butting our heads against a common enemy in these here parts. It's those damned Yanks who come out here acting as if they own every square inch they set foot on. They're a plague on this here land."

"Yes. The time has now come to make war with the Americans."

"I propose a partnership, Two Bulls. Your people and mine. I can supply guns, powder, and lead, and you the warriors." Smythe grinned. "Just like we did back in 1812. Only this time I intend to beat the bloody Americans!"

Gray Feather could hardly believe what he was hearing. Smythe was planning to fight the War of 1812 all over again! The British had lost that struggle, even with all the support that England could send over. How could a single man and a handful of mostly peaceful Indians hope to do any better?

His head was whirling, and he clung tenaciously to consciousness even though he had slumped to the ground. Suddenly the truth occurred to him. Smythe must be insane. His obvious hatred for Americans had addled his brain!

"There was a white man," Two Bulls was saying. Gray Feather heard the words distantly, as if they were coming out of a heavy fog that was playing tricks with the sounds, echoing them at him from several directions. "Where is he?"

Calling Elk said, "The American left before Smythe arrived, but I know where to find his trail."

"Tell me so that I might pursue him and bring back his scalp to hang from my lodge pole."

"No, Two Bulls. You must take the man called Gray Feather back to our village. I will follow this American called Kit Carson. Leave the warriors with me, for you will need no strength in numbers to do what you must do. Gray Feather has lost much blood. He will give you no trouble."

The warriors looked at the wounded Ute slumped pitifully against a tree. Gray Feather blinked sweat from his eyes and saw the look of disappointment come to Two Bulls's face. Then the warrior's face changed as a thought suddenly seemed to steal into his brain. Gray Feather had a sinking feeling that with Two Bulls in charge of taking him back, he'd not make the Flathead village alive.

"It will be as you say, Calling Elk." Two Bulls shot a quick look at Smythe, and the two men shared a secretive grin between themselves. "I will take him back. Stalking Wolf and Hump will come, too, for it looks like he will have to be carried."

"Yes, Hump and Stalking Wolf should help you."

Gray Feather knew that his end had come for sure. Their treachery was written plainly on their faces.

"I will go with them too," Man With Many Horses said suddenly.

"No!" Two Bulls shot back. "We do not require your help."

Gray Feather was verging on unconsciousness, but he forced himself to hang on just a few moments longer. Man With Many Horses stepped up to Two Bulls, standing taller and broader than the surly Flathead warrior. He wore a look of easy confidence, which so suited him. "Gray Feather is my friend. In spite of what he and his white companion are said to have done, it is my place to see that he gets back to the village so that he might have a fair hearing before the council of elders.''

''And you do not think I can bring him back safely?''

''I did not say that,'' Man With Many Horses replied. ''I only wish to accompany my friend and see that his wounds are tended to. And if he needs to be carried, then I will carry him.''

There was no denying that if any carrying need doing, Man With Many Horses was the one most qualified to do it.

Calling Elk said, ''Yes, you too must return with them, Man With Many Horses. The rest of the warriors will come with me.''

Through the fog and the buzzing inside his head, Gray Feather drew in a huge sigh of relief. And even though he could not be sure of it, he had a feeling that Calling Elk had drawn a similar breath. With Man With Many Horses along he would at least make it back alive . . . that is, if the bleeding didn't kill him first.

Consciousness slowly ebbed, voices growing indistinct. In his waning moments Gray Feather made out Smythe's gruff words as he told Calling Elk that he and Marsten would be on their way and wished them luck finding the bloody American. The sound of horses riding away followed, then someone stopped at his side and stood over him, but that was about all that Gray Feather remembered until hours later when he once again regained consciousness—only to discover he had gone from the frying pan into the fire.

* * *

Upon leaving the cave, Kit immediately put Gray Feather and Chief Calling Elk out of his thoughts. He'd done an admirable job of covering his trail, and he knew it would take days for the Flatheads to find them—if not longer. And since Gray Feather appeared to be regaining his strength nicely, Kit turned his thoughts instead to tracking down King George's men.

What would he do once he found them?

Kit half grinned to himself. Maybe he would just walk in and demand a powwow with the Booshway— the brigade captain; the big, peg-legged fellow called Smythe, who had brought in those two murdered warriors.

Following the bearings he'd fixed in his memory the night before, Kit hurried through the forest, always alert for any sound of danger, any odor that might mark the nearness of the camp. At night the glare of a campfire in the middle of a dark forest could be deceptive. It might lie several miles away or only a few dozen yards.

All Kit knew for certain was the direction his inbuilt compass was unerringly indicating.

As he traveled, a part of his brain went over what he already knew about the crimes, which after he had cataloged them he realized were considerable. He knew that so far the Flatheads had seen only the results of the renegades' work; never once had they, or anyone else as far as Kit could determine, witnessed it. He knew that whoever had come through this country had left behind a beaver trap of Hudson's Bay origin, not of Missouri, where a great majority of the American equipment had come from.

But the evidence discovered around the murdered

Flatheads had been distinctly American in origin. A knife, some traps, a couple of rifles. Man With Many Horses had told them these details. Kit's thoughts came to a halt. That part of the story definitely rang a sour note.

A frown deepened on his face. It might be possible for a man to leave a knife behind, and it might even be possible to drop a trap in a hasty moment, especially in the heat of battle . . . but to lose a rifle? That seemed hardly likely. Rifles were just too hard to come by in the wilderness, and too expensive—especially for those free trappers who were not employed by a big eastern company and regularly supplied by them. Unless a rifle was empty and slowing down a man being chased by Indians or beasts, he would *never* leave it behind. It just wasn't done!

Kit pondered the dilemma. Yet somehow, rifles had been dropped, knives left behind, traps found to point the incriminating finger.

A noise brought his pondering to a stop, and his feet as well. At first nothing moved in the forest around him; then to his right and not very far away a bush rustled. Whatever was moving within it was too large to be a man. That left only one creature big enough and likely enough to be rummaging around there.

Kit dropped to his haunches and scooted behind the bole of a tall pine tree. Amid the greenery he caught a glimpse of silver-tipped hair.

"A white bear," he said quietly to himself.

Kit had run up against grizzlies more times than he cared to count. They were an unpredictable lot with dim eyesight. But their poor eyes were more than made up for by their keen sense of smell. There was no telling which way Old Epharim would go if he caught wind of you. Some just turned and ambled away; others plain ignored you. But it was the third kind that Kit worried most about: the cantankerous old sow or the young mother with cubs. Males generally fell into that second category, although there had been exceptions. But a female with cubs was a powder keg with a short fuse.

Kit glanced about for a tree to shinny up real quick if the need arose. He spied a likely candidate nearby, but for now he was content to stay put. If he was lucky this griz would soon be on its way, and then so would Kit. Just the same, he glanced at the nipple of his buffalo gun to make sure a cap was in place and ready.

The last thing he wanted to do, not knowing how far the Englishmen's camp was, was fire his rifle. Kit never liked giving advance notice of his comings or goings, but he readied his rifle anyway. He might not have time to make that tree if this critter decided to become belligerent.

Chapter Eleven

Two Bulls sent Stalking Wolf ahead to alert the village of their arrival and the good news that they had found the chief safe. Secretly, however, he had instructed the warrior to begin stirring up the fires of hatred toward Gray Feather. He wanted to deal with the Ute his way when they reached home, regardless of how vigorously Man With Many Horses protested. And the only way to succeed in that was to win the village over to his side in advance.

Drifting in and out of a half-conscious daze, Gray Feather remembered only bits and pieces of the journey back to the Flathead village. His legs seemed to move automatically—certainly he was no longer in control—and he was vaguely aware that someone was supporting most of his weight. He would have crashed to the ground at once otherwise. At some point during the long walk he lost all connection with the world around him, until some time later when a chorus of angry voices pulled him reluctantly from his deep and peaceful slumber.

Lining both sides of the trail coming into the encampment, men and women jeered at Gray Feather. Someone threw a rock; a woman in tears and clutching a baby to her side ran up wielding a stick. Gray Feather lifted an arm feebly to protect himself, but only Man With Many Horses stepping between them prevented another serious injury. He hustled his dazed friend past the shouts and curses and into the village.

There waiting for them was a band of men.

"Hear me, my brothers," Two Bulls shouted. "We have captured the enemy of our people."

"He is not our enemy," Man With Many Horses protested, but immediately his words were cut off by the jeers of men and women closing in on them.

"This Ute and the white American are the ones who took our chief. The white man has so far eluded us, but Calling Elk is closing in on him. Even so, we have this one. I say we make him pay for his treachery!"

"No," Man With Many Horses shouted. "Calling Elk would not want it so."

"Do we listen to the words of an outsider?" Two Bulls railed.

The people rushed forward, wrenching Gray Feather from Man With Many Horses's grasp. In spite of the warrior's great strength, he could not fight all of the people. They dragged the half-conscious man into the center of the village, where two men fell upon him, binding his wrists and ankles. Another man brought stakes, and in minutes Gray Feather was stretched out on the ground beneath the burning sun.

Someone found a pot of honey and poured the thick, sticky-sweet liquid on his legs, chest, and face. Then everyone backed off to wait and see how long it was going to take the ants to find him.

Honey seeped into the creases of his neck and ran into his armpits. With each stab of pain that wrenched his half-naked body, more gritty soil clung to his back and found its way into his ears. Blinding sunlight glared against his closed eyelids and seared his already aching flesh. In the moments before he lost consciousness, Gray Feather's desperate brain severed the connections with his tortured body and gave him a glimpse of two young boys splashing in a cool mountain stream. It was himself and his friend Little Wanderer. In his mind, Gray Feather sat against a tall tree in its cool shade, watching the boys splashing each other and darting in and out between the boulders.

Inwardly, Gray Feather smiled. He had come home again.

Man With Many Horses stood back, beyond the crowd of villagers who watched with perverted delight as the man staked to the ground burned beneath the merciless sun. Already the honey's sweet enticement had drawn flies, and soon the ants would find it too.

He was aware of someone stepping up behind him. He felt a soft touch upon his arm, and heard, "Come away from here, my husband. There is little you can do to change what is happening."

"He is my friend," Man With Many Horses replied.

"I know." Mary Fawn Hiding stared at the unconscious man and the curious faces of her people. "They are all wondering how long he will endure. And if he will cry out for mercy. If he does cry out, then Two Bulls will end it. See, already he stands near with his war lance."

Man With Many Horses's view shifted toward the warrior and his friends. "I do not understand all of this. Why has Two Bulls this burning hatred for Gray Feather? He is not the one who has brought pain and death to our village. Perhaps it is the Americans who have done these things. But I know Gray Feather. He would not. Even as a boy he was not like the others. Where we would mimic the warriors and play at hunting or at war, Gray Feather would be content to peer long at a bird on a branch, or watch the habits of the fish to learn how they would hide in the deep water where shadows lay. When his father came to take him away to the white world, we all knew that Gray Feather would find so many new things to watch and learn about that he would not miss the mountains."

"But he did come back," she pointed out. "It must have been the longing call of his people and his home that summoned him."

"I have heard it said that Gray Feather returned to teach our people the ways and the language of the white man. But Chief Walkara forbid it and said such knowledge was of no use to a Ute."

"Then I think your chief sees with the eyes of the badger. A leader should have the eyes of an eagle."

Man With Many Horses winced. His wife had spoken with a wisdom that many leaders lacked.

"Come back to our lodge. You cannot help Gray Feather now."

He gently twisted his arm from her grasp. "No. I

will stay with my friend. As boys we made a promise. A vow to always help each other—to be ready to die for the other if need be.''

Mary Fawn Hiding stared at him, concern written on her face. Perhaps, Man With Many Horses wondered, it was something she had heard in the tone of his voice. Or perhaps she already knew him well enough to know what he was thinking.

''You were a boy then. Now you are a man. A man cannot cling to those things which are past.''

''Promises do not remain in the past. They are living spirits. They grow up with the boy and grow old with the man.''

''You asked why Two Bulls hates Gray Feather. Do you not see the truth?''

He gave his wife a blank look. ''What are you talking about?''

Mary Fawn Hiding's lips turned down in an exasperated frown. ''You can read the small signs a deer leaves on the ground, and you look into the sky and say today we will have rain, or tomorrow the snow will fall. But you cannot see what is written in a man's heart even when his actions put it in plain sight. Two Bulls hates Gray Feather not because he is friends with the Americans, but because Gray Feather is *your* friend. It is not him he hates, but it is you, my husband. He hates you because of me.''

''Hate is a strong word. Two Bulls sees me as a threat. But hate? I do not think so.''

She shivered violently and wrapped arms around her waist.

''What is wrong?''

''I do not know. All at once I had a very bad feeling . . . a foreshadowing touch, as my grandmother used to call them." Her view lifted to her husband's face, her voice suddenly intense. "He hates you, and if you give him a chance, he will try to kill you. Be careful what you do. Now, come away from here. I do not want to watch what my people are doing."

He did not wish to upset Mary Fawn Hiding any more than he already had. Reluctantly Man With Many Horses allowed his wife to take his hand and lead him away. But already he had formed a plan to help his friend, and now it was just a matter of waiting until the time was right.

"See, he leaves," Hump said.

Two Bulls watched Man With Many Horses and Mary Fawn Hiding step through the doorway of their lodge. A wave of anger swept over him. It happened whenever he saw the two of them together. Controlling it, he leveled his voice and said, "Man With Many Horses is not one to let this go unchallenged."

Stalking Wolf said, "You still believe that he will attempt to rescue his friend?"

"Yes. He bears watching closely." Two Bulls glanced at Gray Feather, who had regained consciousness and lay squirming in the heat and dirt at his feet. "If his friend survives this day, I think we can expect Man With Many Horses to make an attempt tonight."

Hump gave a short laugh. "If that is the way of it, then I wouldn't worry too much. How many more hours of this can a man endure before he cries out for someone to end his suffering?"

"Perhaps even if he does not cry out, heh?" Stalking Wolf suggested, slanting an eye at the war lance in Two Bulls's fist.

"No. I wish to see him survive into the night . . .

at least long enough for Man With Many Horses to try and rescue him.''

Hump glanced over with sudden understanding in his dark eyes. ''Ah! Now I see why you sent Stalking Wolf ahead to kindle the anger of the people. You were planning all along to lure Man With Many Horses into your snare, to force him to make an attempt at saving his friend. Would it not serve your purpose well if Man With Many Horses should end up dead in the attempt?''

''Would it not be the simplest way to remove the interloper from our village?'' Two Bulls countered.

''And from my cousin's lodge?'' Stalking Wolf suggested.

Two Bulls glared at him. ''You wish it not so yourself?''

''Me?'' Stalking Wolf answered, chuckling nervously beneath Two Bulls's burning stare. ''I was against my cousin joining with the outsider from the beginning. You know that. It is you who should be sharing Mary Fawn Hiding's lodge . . . and her blankets,'' he added with a leering grin.

''And so it will be,'' Two Bulls proclaimed willfully, his knuckles whitening around the shaft of the spear. His narrowed gaze returned to the man staked out beneath the merciless sun. ''Tonight we must be watchful. Tonight we will finally be rid of the interloper.''

The huge grizzly bear crashed through the tangled growth of serviceberry, stopped, lifted its great snout skyward, and sniffed the air. It lumbered forward a few steps and lowered its big head, gazing weakly in the direction Kit was hiding.

Kit cast another glance at his sanctuary tree. He could probably make it if he started now. But running was the worst thing a man could do when facing one of the huge white bears that roamed these mountains. He decided instead to hold his station and wait another few moments to see what the bear's intentions were. Even so, his thumb moved up to the hammer of his rifle. It would be his last resort, but he'd take it if the Old Epharim forced his hand.

The griz roared, took a few lumbering strides in Kit's direction, then stopped, his weak eyes straining for the man his keen nostrils told him was there. He swayed from paw to paw, as if trying to make up his mind, then turned away, padded off a step, stopped, and turned back.

Whal, make up your feeble mind, Kit groused, getting impatient. He glanced again at the tree, but dismissed trying for it. Any movement now was bound to bring the nervous beast down on him.

Old Epharim tasted the air again, then with a shake of its huge head it finally turned its wide rump toward Kit and shambled away.

Kit drew in a long breath and let it out in a rush. He waited another few minutes to make certain the big bruin had really gone for good, then stood, stretching his taut muscles. His internal compass made a couple of swings, settled mentally on a bearing, and he moved on again.

It wasn't long before the faint, telltale odor of wood smoke perfumed the air. Kit's nose was not as sensitive as the nose of the griz he'd just encountered, and he was almost upon the Englishmen's camp before he knew it. Keeping to the thick timber, he stalked the last couple hundred feet to the edge of a clearing and hunkered down.

As far as he could make out, the camp was empty; the men were all off somewhere. But the fire that burned in its center warned Kit that the occupants had only recently departed, and most probably intended to return shortly. At first glance there was nothing unusual about the place. Only one tent had been pitched, and it appeared to hold the men's supplies. A canvas tarpaulin stretching between four trees served as a roof to keep rain off and provided a place to prepare meals and eat. Beneath it two felled trees had been dragged in and faced each other to act as benches. High up one tree was a rope where dry meat hung out of reach of most animals. Scattered about the ground were the men's sleeping blankets, each sitting on an oilcloth groundsheet and covered with a piece of canvas. In one part there stood stacks of beaver, badger, fox, and bear pelts, all pressed into bundles, bound up with rawhide straps, waiting for the trip back to Fort Vancouver. The only other curious feature was a stack of boxes near the edge of camp, covered by another canvas tarpaulin.

The lone tent intrigued Kit. He hadn't come to snoop through the camp, and he didn't know what he would be looking for if he did, but since the place was temporarily abandoned, he decided to take advantage of it. He eased out into the open and dashed the dozen or so steps it took to cover the intervening ground. Inside the tent dappled light coming through the canvas revealed a clutter of items Kit recognized at once to be the usual things men living away from civilization would need. There was a keg of gunpowder, a stack of Hudson's Bay blankets like the kind he'd seen in wide use about Chief Calling Elk's village, another keg filled with glass beads, and a small crate of tin mirrors and bone hair combs.

Obviously, Smythe's fur brigade traded widely with the Indians of this area. Twists of chewing tobacco, traps, bullet molds, bars of lead. Everything a body would need to make do far away from the usual lines of commerce.

Kit frowned, and he was about to leave when a thought occurred to him. He took up one of the beaver traps, searching for the maker's mark.

T. Moore!

It was the very same name that was stamped on the trap he'd found at the vandalized beaver ponds. That didn't prove anything, of course, except that the Englishmen had worked that pond sometime before it had been broken open. But it presented some curious possibilities. . . .

A sound wrenched Kit from his thoughts. He stepped out the door in time to spot the flash of a red shirt through the trees. The camp keepers were coming back!

Chapter Twelve

The last thing Kit wanted was for Smythe to catch him snooping around his camp. Kit glanced for a place to hide—at least until he knew for certain who the men were. He had only a second to make a decision. He dove behind the stack of crates covered with a tarp and scurried out of sight. The voices of the returning men reached his ears as they strode back into camp. Kit picked up the thread of their conversation halfway through.

"... the others with 'im," a man with a thick Cockney accent was saying. "William's a strange duck, 'e is. Likes to be alone all the time."

"He didn't seem to mind it that Warrington and Hagman went along, now did he, mate?" the second man said, his accent not quite as thick, his voice much deeper.

Kit sidled up against one of the long crates, as quiet as a mouse at Sunday services.

'' 'E weren't all that pleased with it, either.''

"Ah," the deeper voice replied, "you can't blame the men. We've been a long time away from the comforts of home, we have.''

A brief chuckle. ''Ye mean the comforts of a sweet lass's bosom, don't ye?''

A deeper laugh. ''That too, mate. And a pint of whiskey, I might add.''

"Well, anyway, the boys should be getting back here directly. Suppose I ought to stir up the fire some and get a bit o' that elk meat roasting that Miles shot yesterday.''

"When do you reckon Smythe and Marsten will be getting in?''

"No telling. Smythe's a peculiar one, 'e is. I never 'ave met the likes o' 'im. 'E says one thing, then does the other. 'E's unpredictable, 'e is. Makes me skin prickle all over. Far as I'm concerned, 'e can stay away forever.''

Kit's ears perked up with the mention of the brigade leader's name.

"He sure does hate them Yanks, doesn't he?'' the second man added.

"The man's obsessed. 'E's going to get us all scalped if 'e don't mind his p's and q's. Say, reckon 'e come across another savage and that's what's keeping 'im?''

"No telling. One thing's for certain, Calling Elk's got a brain and eyes. Smythe's walking a fine rope, he is. And if he ain't careful that rope's going to break, and like Jack, we're all going to go tumbling after.''

There was a long pause, then the man with the deep voice continued. ''You know, James, I've heard Mc-Loughlin say more than once he wished he could draw a line across this country and keep all the Americans from crossing over it. But I don't think he had in mind going about it the way Smythe is.''

''No, there'll be hell to pay if McLoughlin ever finds out what Smythe is up to out here, away from the watchful eye of the Crown.''

Deep Voice gave a brief laugh. ''Well, it ain't going to be me telling on him, no sir.''

Cockney agreed. ''No sir, me neither. Did ye see the way 'e run Port through with that sword of 'is? I tell you, Roger, the man's got ice in 'is veins, not blood. 'E's more animal than human.''

Kit thought he heard regret in the other man's voice when he said, ''Smythe wasn't always that way, James. But over the years a change has come over him. At one time he was a right pleasant chap to be around. But after the war when the Treaty of Ghent was signed, and with Napoleon's invasion of France and all, and little hope that the Crown would try to negotiate a treaty more favorable to England, Smythe was devastated. He felt that he'd sacrificed his body to a failed cause and it was all downhill from that, I'm afraid.''

''But that was years ago!''

''Nearly twenty,'' Deep Voice agreed.

''A long time to carry so much hatred in 'is heart, I say.''

''Mmm. Well, we all have our little battles to fight. Smythe is fightin' his the only way he knows how.''

"And if the Company ever finds out what 'e's been up to out here, they'll skin his hide, they will."

"Who's going to tell 'em, James?"

Cockney gave a laugh. "Not me, no sir."

Hidden under the tarp behind the crates, Kit heard a third voice hail the camp.

Cockney, the one Deep Voice called James, shouted back, "It's about time ye boys got back. I'm just putting some food over the fire. Got coffee in the pot and fresh water just carried from the creek."

From the sound of it, four or five men joined the two already there, but Kit dared not poke his head out to count them. Instead he listened to their voices, cataloging them that way. As the camp livened up, it began to look as if he was going to be stuck there at least until the sun went down and darkness gave him the cover he needed to get away. Well, he had plenty of time. Gray Feather was safely tucked away in the cave, so he didn't have to worry about him. There was nowhere he had to be, and he'd already learned more from what he had overheard than he had expected—enough to practically confirm his suspicions. Only one question remained unanswered as far as he was concerned.

Half listening now to the two or three different conversations being carried on, Kit turned his attention to the wooden crates that, like he, were covered over by this tarp. They showed no markings to indicate what they might contain. They were of crude construction, perhaps five feet long and fourteen or eighteen inches deep. The tops were hinged by simple leather straps, and there were no locks, only leather hasps held in place by wooden pegs. Curiosity being one of Kit's weaknesses, he silently wiggled the peg from of one of the hasps. With great care he lifted the lid six inches—all the clearance he had before bumping into the heavy material above his head.

The crate held straw. At least that was all that Kit saw at first. Reaching inside, he worked his hand through the dry, rustling material until his fingers contacted something hard. Kit identified it at once by feel. A rifle. That wasn't surprising, considering all the cheap London Fusils he'd seen in the Flathead village. If Smythe was supplying Calling Elk's village with them, then certainly he would keep a stock on hand.

A thought suddenly flashed through his brain.

What if they weren't London Fusils?

With infinite care, Kit slowly lifted the rifle from its bed of straw. Through the gap of the open lid, it came into view. Kit's eyes widened at what he had discovered, and all at once the answer to that last nagging question was clear.

If he were able to search the crates closer, he'd not be at all surprised to turn up a few Green River knives, and perhaps an American trap or two.

He wanted to give a shout of elation, but contented himself instead with a wide, satisfied grin as he quietly returned the piece and refitted the hasp and peg.

If the white man's version of the place of torment where evil men go in the life hereafter was right, then Gray Feather figured that he'd just had a little taste of it. Gratefully, though, the slanting sunlight was now low enough that the lodges cast their shadows across the ground, and most important, from his point of view, across himself. His body had turned into a mass of blisters, and his skin stung as if pricked by hundreds of fiery needles.

The ants and the horseflies had done their work well.

He'd been unconscious on and off most of the day, but with the cooling of evening he'd awakened, and awareness of his pain came back with a vengeance. And slowly he became aware of another annoyance, a huge thirst that throttled his throat.

Most of the watchers had left, but a few remained, standing in groups, passing the time sociably with each other, occasionally slanting an eye toward the suffering man and perhaps wondering if particular throes of agony might not signal his demise, or grow into a plea for someone to put him out of his misery.

Not just yet! Gray Feather thought, marshaling his resolve to live. *I'll not give you that satisfaction yet!*

But how much more of this could he endure?

He licked his lips, hardly feeling them through his tongue, which seemed to be made more of shriveled moccasin leather than of flesh and muscle. His body cried out for water. But would anyone care?

Turning his head toward the nearest cluster of men, Gray Feather tried to speak. His voice came out in a low rasp that even he hardly heard. He tried again.

"Water."

This time one of the men looked over. He spoke to his companion and everyone stopped talking, more curious than helpful.

"Water," he tried again.

Only interested stares. No one made a move.

"Water!" he managed to cry more loudly.

"Perhaps the rain gatherer will hear your request and bring clouds overhead and let down his rain," one of them quipped. They all laughed as they glanced at the darkening sky in mock anticipation.

"The rain gatherer must be sleeping," another noted after a few moments of chuckling and neck craning.

"Some water, please," Gray Feather implored.

Still no one moved.

Gray Feather shut his eyes and tried to force back his ravenous thirst. Distantly, he heard a commotion coming from the crowd, but he had no energy to waste to determine its cause. Footsteps stopped near his head. Someone sat beside him. Gray Feather opened an eye. It was Man With Many Horses.

"I have brought you a drink, my brother," he said soberly.

"No!" someone shouted. "Give him no water."

With the suddenness of lightning, Man With Many Horses was on his feet. "I will give my friend water to drink, and I challenge any man here who wishes to prevent me from doing this."

The ex–Ute warrior was not a man to trifle with, and no one volunteered to go up against him. His size alone was enough to deter it, but with the glare of white-hot emotion in his eyes, a man would have been a fool to have taken up his challenge.

"Two Bulls, what do you say about this?" one of the warriors asked, quickly transferring the problem to the other man's shoulders.

Man With Many Horses wheeled and narrowed his gaze at the smaller warrior. Two Bulls stopped two paces from him, resting the end of his war lance upon the ground with a fist wrapped about the shaft near its point. If the pose was meant as a threat, it had little effect upon Man With Many Horses.

"You challenge me?"

"No," Two Bulls replied. Then, raising his voice, he continued, "No man here will stop you from giving water to this killer of our people who you call *friend.*"

A murmur rippled through the crowd. Could it be that Two Bulls was showing mercy toward Gray Feather? Or was he simply cowering before Man With Many Horses's prowess?

"There is much poison between us, Two Bulls," Man With Many Horses said evenly. "Everyone knows of it, and they know why. Your bitterness is because Mary Fawn Hiding chose me over you."

Two Bulls's mouth compressed into a thin hard line.

"Because her father chose your *gifts* over mine," he answered. "I did not possess a great number of horses, and it was horses that Tall Bear desired. Mary Fawn Hiding would have been my wife if you had not showed up, interloper!"

"Then your vengeance should be against me, Two Bulls. Not this man. No one has shown that it was he, or his friend, the American, who killed our brothers."

"It was the American who took our chief!" Two Bulls turned toward the crowd, raising his voice. "Do we need any further proof?" he demanded, arousing their cries of approval.

Man With Many Horses saw that he faced minds that were already made up and would not easily be swayed. "Calling Elk will not be pleased," he said, then, holding a water-filled gourd, knelt by Gray Feather's side and gently raised his head.

"Drink deeply, my friend, but not too fast."

Gray Feather gulped it down in spite of Man With Many Horses's advice.

"Hold. If you do not take small sips it will make you sick."

The water revitalized Gray Feather a little. When he had drunk all that he could for the moment, Man With Many Horses lowered his head to the ground.

"How . . . how long will they keep me here?" he asked, licking parched and blistered lips.

"Until you cross over, my friend, or until our chief returns and puts a stop to this."

Gray Feather managed a weak grin. "Or until Kit comes looking for me."

"It will be better if he does not come back here. The people will not be as kind to him."

"Kind?" Gray Feather groaned. "If this is kindness, I hate to see cruelty."

"Don't talk now. Save your strength."

"Why should I bother? It will all be the same in the end."

Man With Many Horses glanced quickly around, then picked up the drinking gourd. Catching Gray Feather's eye, he dropped his voice to barely a whisper and said, "Rest now, my friend. Later tonight, look for me. Make no sound to anger Two Bulls. Give him no excuse to kill you just yet." Standing, Man With Many Horses swept the crowd with a dark and angry glare, then forced his way past Two Bulls and returned to his lodge.

Gray Feather played his friend's words over in his head, clinging to the thread of hope that he'd heard in them as a shipwrecked man would clamber atop a broken spar in a shark-infested sea.

Closing his eyes, he was instantly asleep.

Chapter Thirteen

"He moves like the wind," Mountain Buck declared with both vexation and admiration in his voice. "He leaves little behind to follow."

"But only a ghost passes without leaving a trace," Calling Elk reminded him, "and this man is not a spirit, but flesh."

After parting company with Smythe earlier that day, and sending the four men back to the village with Gray Feather as their prisoner, Calling Elk had led the rest of his warriors back to the cave where he had been held captive.

They spent the better part of the afternoon sorting through the several tracks leading away from the hiding place—one turned out to be the trace that Kit had left when he had gone back to the village the previous night. Finally they had hit upon the way Kit had gone that morning. Still, the going was slow. As Mountain

Buck had said, Kit left very little behind to follow. But they pressed on, sending runners ahead to flank either side so that the party, which for the most part was mounted on ponies, made sure the trace was not lost.

When evening arrived, drawing its dark blanket over them, Calling Elk pondered the problem of finding the man he believed had caused the death of at least two of his braves. Perhaps he had been the one behind all the murders as well. But then, just when he was certain he had the right man, a bit of doubt would creep into a corner of his brain and sit there grinning at him. Something did not ring true. Kit Carson had spared his life when, any way you looked at it, killing him would have been the most practical and sensible thing to do.

"Do we make camp for the night?" Mountain Buck asked when Calling Elk had lapsed into a long, introspective silence.

The question pulled the chief from his thoughts. "The trace is difficult to follow, yet it is less than one day old. Tomorrow will it be any easier to follow?"

"No. Time makes it more difficult."

Calling Elk nodded his head. "Yes, and so does the darkness. We are given two hard choices."

"The moon smiles full upon the face of the land tonight," Mountain Buck pointed out.

"Ah, but the trees stand tall and turn back its smile."

"I can follow a thread of smoke through the lodges of the underworld spirits," Mountain Buck boasted. "Following this white man's trace beneath a big moon is child's play to me."

Calling Elk knew that the men were awaiting his decision. The men were all good trackers, and no one wanted to give up the trail now, not when they had searched so long and hard to locate it in the first place. No one wanted the American to slip away. Calling Elk came to a decision.

"We will continue tonight."

Kit had waited until the darkness was complete, then had lingered on a little while longer, hidden beneath the tarp, waiting for the campsite to quiet down so that he could slip away undetected. He might have made it at that moment, but why tempt fate when another hour would assure his safe departure?

He had come to learn through the talk that he'd overheard that the brigade leader, Smythe, and another fellow named Marsten had departed that morning to explore new beaver ground to the west. Everyone had expected them back sometime today. But now with the night full upon them, some of the trappers were predicting that Smythe would not return until morning.

Kit was vaguely disappointed. He wanted to learn more about the big, one-eyed, peg-legged brigade leader, and what better way than to listen to the man speak and be spoken to? In his tight hiding place, Kit shifted upon the hard ground and thought once again about slipping away. But there really was no hurry. He had all night, and Gray Feather was safely hidden inside the small cave with Calling Elk. Kit grinned into the darkness, thinking about the Flathead Chief and Gray Feather together for all these hours. He reckoned that the chief probably already knew more about Shakespeare than any other Flathead alive. Not that it would have made any sense to Calling Elk, but talking about English literature was one of Gray Feather's great joys in life.

"Hello the camp!" a voice echoed out of the dark forest.

Kit glanced at the dark sheet over him and was tempted to stick his head out to see who this new arrival was. His question was answered almost immediately.

"Why, it's Smythe," one of the men said, surprised.

"Told you he'd be back tonight, Tolly. Looks like you owe me half a quid," another man commented dryly.

Sounds of horses emerged from the night, and Kit listened to the men dismounting and others gathering around.

"We were beginning to wonder if ye and Marsten were going to make it back tonight," said a voice that Kit had earlier tagged as belonging to one of the camp keepers.

"Had us a little delay," Smythe announced. "But it turned out be a stroke of fine luck, boys." Kit's ears perked up when he heard the deep satisfaction in the brigade leader's voice.

"What are you talking about?" someone asked.

"Some coffee," Smythe demanded.

"Got a pot of coffee on the fire," the camp keeper offered.

There was the soft clatter of tin cups, then another man asked, "Wot are you all smug about, Alex? You look like you found yourself a mountain of pearls and gold over yonder."

"It wasn't gold wot we found," a new voice boasted proudly.

Kit ticked off a list of names he had been keeping in his brain and discovered that the only man he had not yet tagged with a voice was someone the other men had referred to as "Marsten."

"Well, are you gonna tell us, Alex, before we all grow old waiting?"

Smythe's deep voice was unmistakable. It carried with it a ring of authority. "It happened right after we left here this morning," he began. "We were about five miles west of here when I heard a sound. Marsten and me crept over to take a look, and what did we see?"

They waited while Smythe let the silence stretch out uncomfortably long.

"The American!" Smythe roared, laughing.

"The American?" someone asked. "You mean the one who slipped out from Calling Elk's village?"

"The very same. And know who he had with him?" Before anyone had ventured an opinion, Smythe said, "Calling Elk himself!"

"The chief? Blind me!" the camp keeper declared. "What did ye do?"

"We trailed the bloke," Marsten said. "Trailed him is wot we did, and he led us straight to the second fellow, a Ute who was all busted up from a bullet wot he took while making his getaway."

Kit's easy feeling of a few minutes before evaporated and was immediately replaced by alarm. He listened to Smythe explain how they had met up with the Flathead warriors and put Gray Feather in their charge. At least his friend had been alive when Smythe last saw him, Kit thought at first. But what the brigade leader said next made Kit's blood turn to ice.

"I caught that Injun's eye, the one called Two Bulls. There was murder in it, even though the chief made it plain he didn't want the Ute killed just yet. I wouldn't be at all surprised if his hair's already parted company with his scalp."

The trappers laughed.

Hidden away in the shadows beneath the canvas tarp, Kit frowned.

He'd been careless!

Gray Feather had been taken captive, and all this time Kit had whiled away the afternoon when his friend was in dire need of his help. Gray Feather might even be dead by now, if Smythe's reading of Two Bulls was correct.

His worry settled like an elephant upon his chest. He had sought out these British trappers to learn more about the stories of Americans ravaging the Flathead territory . . . to possibly stop a war. But the importance of all that paled now compared to the news he'd just heard. Above all else, he had to make his way away from there and hurry back to Calling Elk's village before it was too late . . . if it wasn't too late already.

He hadn't a moment to lose. Kit elbowed his way to the edge of the canvas and peeked beneath it. The trappers were together near the fire, not looking his way. Now would be as good a time as any to make his escape. Once the decision was made, Kit wasted no time. He crawled the rest of the way out and prayed that no one would glance his way as he inched across the ground toward the safety of the trees.

But one of the men did look his way.

"G' blind me! Look!"

The trappers craned their necks around, every one

of them. Kit had lost what little bit of secrecy he was hoping for. Instantly he leaped to his feet and darted into the forest. Right on his heels were half a dozen men, bearing down on him, quickly closing the short distance.

There was no time to be clever, no time to try to elude these Englishmen. He had only one chance, and that was to outdistance them. Sounds of pursuit were all around. The crashing of men coming through the brush to his left sounded too near for comfort; the snap of branches to his right crackled only yards away.

"There he is!" someone shouted. It sounded to Kit as if the man was right behind him.

Kit dodged, swerved, and ducked under low branches. A flash to his left and the thunder of a rifle shot made him wince as a shower of tree bark sprayed his cheek. His own rifle was nearly useless, since he could not pause to aim—and aim at what? He had only one shot.

Kit plunged on.

A wall of trees and rocks rose suddenly before him and forced him to swerve left. Then, out of the darkness, a root in his path reached out and snagged his foot. Kit reeled forward, tried to stop his forward stumble, and smacked his head into a tree. Stunned, he rolled onto his back. The starry sky and the bright moon above were jiggling as if the dark heavens were a bowl of gelatin. He shook off the dizziness and pushed himself up onto his knees.

"Hey, boys. This way!" someone shouted nearby.

Footsteps echoed in his still-dazed mind as a man suddenly leaped into sight. Kit sprang for the man like a cornered mountain lion, fingers wrapping about his throat like a vise as his weight carried them both down. Kit snatched the butcher knife from his belt and lifted it high.

Someone grabbed his fist from behind. More hands locked onto his arms and wrists, dragging him back. Kit struggled against them but was easily overpowered. They dragged him to his feet and wrenched his arms achingly behind his back.

"G' blind me if it ain't the Yank!"

"By Godfry, you're right, Marsten," a burly fellow said, squinting hard at Kit.

His head was still buzzing from the blow, but even so, Kit could hear the uneven gait of another man coming toward them. "So, it's you," a deep voice boomed, mildly amazed. The owner of the voice stepped into view, his single eye narrowing down at Kit.

"Smythe," Kit wheezed between deep, gulping breaths.

"Ah, you know me?"

"Know *of* you." Kit tried unsuccessfully to break loose of their grasp.

"What were you doing nosing around my camp, Yank?"

He was about to turn the question around and demand what Smythe was doing carrying around a supply of American rifles. But he managed to hold his tongue at the last moment. It would not serve his purpose to let on too soon what he had learned. If Smythe thought him ignorant of his treachery, he might just yet be able to talk his way out of this predicament.

"I stumbled on your camp by accident," he said glibly, grinning as if it were all just a big mistake.

With a sudden whisper of steel against steel,

140

Smythe's saber leaped from its scabbard and its sharp point lurched forward, touching Kit's Adam's apple.

"And I'm the King's favorite son, I am," Smythe growled. Muffled laughter rippled around him. "Now, you Yankee bastard, I'll ask one more time, and if I don't get the truth out of you, I'll pluck out your neck bones one bloody vertebra at a time. What were you doing nosing around my camp?"

A couple of choices raced through Kit's head as he stared down at the short sword glinting dully in the faint moonlight, digging alarmingly deep into his skin. If he told Smythe about finding the rifles, the glaring mountain pirate would run him through where he stood. And if he told a lie—unless it was a very convincing lie—the results would be the same.

Kit gulped.

He had no choice but to tell this man what he demanded to know. The truth was all Smythe had asked for, and the truth was what Kit would give him . . . and not one word more.

Chapter Fourteen

Gray Feather's eyes snapped open. His back ached where a stone upon which he was lying had dug into his spine. His side burned with the fierce pain, and he imagined in his weakened state that someone had run him through with a red-hot poker. His skin prickled in a hundred places where voracious ants had taken a taste of his hide while trailing through the honey, which now, in the shivering coolness of a mountain night, had solidified in every wrinkle and fold of his skin.

He lay there, aching every way possible, including a tremendous thirst that had overtaken him sometime during the night. But remarkably, his mind was suddenly clear. The sleep, in spite of the bugs and stone, had brought some vigor back to his suffering body.

But something had awakened him!

Although reared most of his life in the civilized

world of New England, Gray Feather still possessed the uncanny inbred wariness of a man born to the wild—a sixth sense honed to a keen edge in his early years with the Ute Indians. Now it instinctively took over. He lay unmoving, even though that irritating rock beneath him urged him to shift position just a little.

He didn't.

Ears straining against the quiet night sounds, Gray Feather sorted though them: a coyote in the distance, an owl somewhere far off, a . . . *footstep?*

"I know you are awake," came a voice that Gray Feather recognized at once. "Do not make a sound, my friend." A knife sliced through the cords holding his hands. Man With Many Horses moved next to his feet, and in seconds he was free.

"Quickly, before you are discovered missing."

As Man With Many Horses helped Gray Feather to his feet the pain in his side exploded. The torment was almost overwhelming. He had nearly forgotten how badly a person could hurt. But it was there yet, reminding him that he was not a well man. With his friend's help, Gray Feather hobbled behind one of the lodges. In its shadows Man With Many Horses paused to gave him a drink of water.

"There is no time to rest. We must make our escape at once. Two Bulls has appointed men to come often to observe you." Man With Many Horses spoke softly near his ear, for sounds tend to carry far in the night. "I have watched a man come three times tonight. He has just left. That should give us a good start."

Gray Feather tried to straighten up. The best he could manage was a hunched-forward bend, like an old man. "Let's go," he said, gritting his teeth against the pain.

With Man With Many Horses's help, he made for the edge of the village and the forest that lay a little way beyond an open, grassy swale. Before starting across the moonlit stretch of ground, Man With Many Horses halted and glanced quickly around, as if looking for something or someone. In a few moments Gray Feather saw a dark figure separate from the deeper shadow of one of the lodges and come quickly toward them, hunched low to the ground, carrying something. It was Mary Fawn Hiding, carrying Man With Many Horses's musket and a hunting bag.

He took them from her. "Go back to our lodge now, quickly, before you are seen," he whispered urgently.

"Be careful, my husband." Her simple words carried with them the agony of separation, the dread of loss. Mary Fawn Hiding stretched out a hand and gently touched Man With Many Horses's cheek.

He cupped her hand in his own, held it briefly against his face, then pushed it away. "Now, leave. Quickly."

She obeyed, but Gray Feather could not help but notice the reluctance that seemed to hold her there. It was as if an unseen rope was tugging her back to him. She finally broke its grip on her and left them.

"Now, my friend," Man With Many Horses said, "we will cross to the trees, and once in the forest I will take you to a safe place that I know of."

"You won't be able to come back to the village once they find out."

Man With Many Horses gave him a quick but confident grin. "Not right away, at least. But once Calling Elk returns and learns of Two Bulls's treachery, I think it will be all right. We waste time talking. We will have to move like rabbits. Are you ready?''

"Ready as I will ever be."

Man With Many Horses made one more sweep of the wide track of open land they had to cross. Not seeing anyone, he lifted Gray Feather by the arm and started him across it.

Gray Feather silently cursed the revealing moonlight and his own slow, hobbled gait, but neither could be helped. He glanced over his shoulder, and his hopes began to mount as the village receded and each painful step carried him closer to freedom. Maybe, just maybe, he would make it away from there and the misery Two Bulls had put him through.

But in spite of all his hopes, a part of his brain was warning him that the escape was going too well. It was too easy. Ahead the dark forest loomed nearer. They were almost there.

Man With Many Horses steered him toward a clump of dark trees standing out from the forest. As they got closer, something about the trees made Gray Feather's hair bristle. Two of the trees looked particularly short, as if they were only stumps with their tops chopped off. But it wasn't until he and Man With Many Horses were within two dozen feet of them that Gray Feather suddenly realized the truth. Man With Many Horses understood at the same moment, but by then it was too late.

One of the short trees moved, becoming suddenly less stumplike and more manlike. The other stump became animated too.

Instantly the pair of old friends came to a stop. Man With Many Horses glanced around and started off in a new direction. But a third man stepped from the edge of the forest, bringing the two to a halt for a second time.

"I suspected you would try something like this, interloper," Two Bulls said as he strode from the forest's edge with his musket pointed at them.

The two standing figures whom Gray Feather had mistaken in the dark for tree stumps turned out to be Hump and Stalking Wolf. Somehow he wasn't surprised.

"Once again you have proved that your treachery is beyond words," Man With Many Horses said, stepping in front of Gray Feather.

Gray Feather grimaced and tried to straighten up without the aid of his friend's arm. If he was to face death, he'd do it standing tall and proud.

"My treachery?" Two Bulls exclaimed. "It is you who is helping this murderer of our brothers—*my* brothers—to escape. I have guessed all along where *your* true loyalties lie."

While putting himself between Gray Feather and Two Bulls, Man With Many Horses had stealthily removed a knife from his waist and secretly passed it back to his friend. Gray Feather at once transferred the knife to the small of his back, beneath his belt, as Stalking Wolf and Hump fell in on either side of Two Bulls.

Man With Many Horses said, "Many times have I declared that this man did not murder *our* brothers. But you have ears that do not hear the truth. They are deafened by the bitterness that dwells in your heart. Is it justice for you to seek your revenge against me by torturing this man because he is my friend? Because I won the heart of the woman you desired? A

woman you could never have made to love you? Even
if you had owned as many horses at the stars above,
her father would not have given Mary Fawn Hiding
to you. He has spoken of this to me many times.''

''It's a lie!'' Two Bulls roared, shaking with rage.
His finger reached for the trigger. ''She would have
had me if you had not come into our village. It is you
who poisoned her heart toward me!''

''No, it was not I,'' Man With Many Horses said
evenly. ''It was the jealousy within your own heart
that did the poisoning. You managed to cleverly hide
your corruption before I arrived, but my coming revealed your true character to everyone, like cutting
open a choice apple only to find that a worm had
eaten out its center and had made it rotten. She saw
it plainly then, just as many of the people in our village have seen it. Once the decay was exposed, Mary
Fawn Hiding wanted nothing more to do with you.''

''All that has happened to me, it is your fault, interloper!''

''We each make our own ways, Two Bulls. The
path you walk today is one you laid out yourself by
the paths that you chose before. I had nothing to do
with it. Just as you had nothing to do with the path I
now walk. Everyone comes to crossroads and everyone must choose which way he will go. That is all.''

''Is that so?'' Two Bulls sneered, his voice suddenly taking on a chilling edge. ''If that is true, then
tell me, interloper, which path did you walk which
has led you here, to this moment—to the door of the
death keeper's lodge?''

Gray Feather heard the change come to Two
Bulls's voice. All at once he knew what would happen next. ''No, Two Bulls, don't do it—''

Gray Feather tried to shove Man With Many Horses aside, but he moved too slowly. The musket's echoing roar shattered the peaceful night and the tall Ute reeled back, hands clutching his breast.

Gray Feather stared unbelievingly at his friend sprawled upon the grass. In the night the dark flow of blood began to spread out upon Man With Many Horses's chest. Rage replacing shock, Gray Feather wheeled around, ignoring the searing pain of the bullet wound in his side. Drawing the knife from his belt, he lurched unsteadily at the warrior.

But Two Bulls was quicker. He snapped the butt of his musket up and drove it alongside Gray Feather's skull, instantly dropping him in his tracks.

"You've killed them both," Hump said, worried.

Through an enveloping fog, Gray Feather heard the words as if Hump were speaking softly at the far end of a tunnel.

"No, only the interloper," Two Bulls replied, his words coming in short, strained bursts.

"What will you say when the elders come? Look, already your shot has awakened the village. Here they come now."

"I will tell them that the interloper's loyalty was with the prisoner. I stopped him from freeing the murderer, and when he tried to use his rifle, I shot him."

That's not what happened! Gray Feather thought, hovering on the brink of unconsciousness. *You murdered him in cold blood.*

"And this one?" It was Stalking Wolf's voice. He bent, and Gray Feather felt a hand momentarily cup his nose. "He still breathes."

"Perhaps now, but he won't by morning," Two Bulls said confidently.

148

Gray Feather heard hurried footsteps approaching, a woman's muffled cry, a man's voice . . . and then nothing at all.

"Wot? G' blind me, Gov'nor. You don't believe this bloke, do you?" Marsten complained. He was plainly disappointed that Smythe had not promptly run Kit through with his sword. "You don't believe all this bloody rubbish about him just wanting to talk to you?"

Smythe held Kit for a long, tense moment beneath his piercing, single-eye stare. Slowly he withdrew his saber and said, "It's such a simple answer that it just could be true. And this fellow doesn't look like he's simpleminded." Smythe said to Kit, "You aren't, are you, Yank?"

"I'm not what?" Kit asked.

"Simpleminded."

It was a question that needed no reply.

Marsten cursed and whined, "Let me shoot the bloke now! We don't need him for nothing."

"When the time is right. For now, bring him into camp. He says he came to talk with me, so we'll have us a little chat. Then you can shoot him."

Marsten was only marginally appeased by Smythe's promise. He was plainly aching to shoot someone, and he wanted to do it now. Kit was relieved that Smythe had at least some control over the wild-eyed fellow.

With a man on each side of him, Kit was pulled roughly along toward the firelight flickering through the trees. Once inside the camp circle they released him, but with three rifles pointed in his direction, Kit didn't figure he'd have any better luck making a break now than he had the first time he tried it.

Their firelight lit only a small patch of ground, leaving the rest of the camp site in shadows. Kit was aware of the men backing up and leaving him standing alone near the fire. They were making him a clear and easy target for any of their rifles.

Smythe stepped into view, scowling through his shaggy beard. His black patch and peg leg reminded Kit of the dangerous characters he'd heard of in tales told by those ex–seafaring men who had traded a wave-washed deck for the back of a horse and a beaver trap.

"By what name are you called?" Smythe demanded.

Kit's head was still reeling from the blow it had received. "My name's Christopher Carson, but generally I'm just called Kit."

"Well, Mr. Christopher Carson, you said you came here to talk to me. It's such a simple statement that I'm inclined to believe it's the truth. I usually shoot strangers who come snooping around my camp, but I'll hear you out first . . . then I'll shoot you. So start talking."

Kit had already found the answers to his questions in the crates hidden away beneath the tarpaulin. But if he told Smythe that, this reprieve would turn out to be a quick walk down a very short plank. And glancing around him at the shadowy figures standing just beyond the reach of the firelight, Kit mused that the waters below were thick with sharks.

He had to think fast. He shook his head to clear some of the lingering wool. He licked his lips. They felt mighty dry from not having tasted water most of the day.

"I could sure use something to wet my whistle. I've not had much to drink today."

"What do I look like, an innkeeper? This ain't a pub for wayward travelers," Smythe snapped. "You're stalling, Carson."

Kit's senses were beginning to return now, and he grinned amiably to try to put Smythe at ease. "Whal, I see you're not a man of many words. I don't much go in for small talk myself, Mr. Smythe, so I reckon I'll get right down to business. I seen you bringing in those two unfortunate Flatheads the other day." That was true enough . . . so far.

"So, what of it?" In spite of his bluster, there was a note of wary concern in Smythe's voice.

"It was the proper thing to do. The Christian thing to do! I'd have done the same if I'd found those poor fellows," Kit said, feeling his way along this train of thought. He was making it all up as he went, and he didn't want to go too fast.

"What are you getting at, Carson?"

"Whal, it's why I come looking for you, Mr. Smythe. You seem to have a friendly way with the chief."

"Calling Elk? We deal some."

Kit laughed, hoping to dull Smythe's wary edge. "You must deal a lot, judging by all those muskets and blankets I seen in my short visit."

Smythe's bushy eyebrows narrowed. "You're still dancing around the point, Carson. What business do you think you've got with me?"

"It's like this. That Flathead chief has got it into his thick skull that me and my partner had something to do with all them murders. And he thinks we busted up them beaver dams, too. Whal, the plain truth of the matter is, we was just passing through and somehow managed to stumble into this mess. We had nothing at all to do with that mischief.''

"Is that a fact?" Smythe gave a small grin. "I think I see what you're getting at, Carson."

"You do?" Kit was mildly surprised. He wasn't certain that *he* even knew what he was getting at yet.

"You want me to have a powwow with the chief so that he'll spare your mangy hide, and that of your Injun friend. Ain't that right?"

It sounded like a good enough yarn to him, and Kit was willing to go along with it. "Gray Feather and me, we would sure be much obliged if you would talk to him." He'd managed to put Smythe off his guard, but the noose was still around his neck.

All at once Smythe exploded in a deep, rumbling laugh. He glanced around at the men standing there. "Didya hear that, boys? This Yank wants me to talk Calling Elk into sparing his hide!"

The men chuckled. Marsten said, "Can I shoot the bloke now, Gov'nor?"

"Not yet." Smythe turned back to Kit. "You're about as dumb as dirt, ain't you, Yank? I reckon you must be simpleminded after all, if you think I'd try to shuck Calling Elk off of your trail!" His amusement turned to sudden fury, his deep voice bellowing at Kit. "What makes you think I'd help you?"

Before Kit could reply, Smythe raged, "You want to know the truth, Yank? Well, since I'm gonna let Marsten blow your fool head off in another minute, I'll tell you. It was me who done them savages in. Yeah, that's right. It was me. And you want to know why?" He pointed at his patched eye. "See this? And this peg? I lost 'em both to Yankee cannon fire at Frenchtown.''

Like striking a flame in a dark room, Kit suddenly understood. The battle at Frenchtown had occurred during the War of 1812. He thought it incredible that a man could carry a grudge for so many years, but he had heard of such things before. Old Hugh Glass had hauled a mighty big hatred around for over a year after two men whom he'd trusted had left him alone and weaponless to die in the wilderness. Hugh had somehow managed to crawl out of that fix and hunt the men down. But in the end he forgave them. Hugh was not crazy, but Kit suspected that the same could not be said of Smythe.

"That was more than twenty years ago, Smythe," Kit said.

"Plenty of time to plan how I was going to strike back at you bloody Yanks!" he roared.

Smythe was crazy! Crazy with revenge—revenge that had seethed within him for nearly a quarter of a century. It was also quite clear to Kit that he was not going to be able to talk his way out of this fix. Smythe was becoming more enraged as the moments passed. The only way left to Kit now was to feed the man's rage and hope that it would distract the trappers long enough for him to make a break.

Kit *had* to keep the man talking.

"So you killed the Flatheads, broke apart those beaver dams, and shot game that you never intended to use. Then you figured out a way to pin the blame on us Americans. And you figured that that would be your way of paying us back for England having lost the war?"

Smythe was shaking when he blurted, "This land was all ours at one time. Our trapping grounds until you Americans came! It's not enough you took everything east of the Mississippi. No, you want it all, and someday you'll have it all, from one bloody coast to the other! But not if I can stop you!''

Kit was running out of time. In desperation he said, ''That's why you brought along all those crates of American rifles? So that when you murdered one of the Indians, you could show Calling Elk something American to convince him that we did it.''

The mention of the crates knocked Smythe momentarily off his stride. He blinked, glanced at the tarp-covered pile, then returned his piercing gaze to Kit. ''That's right, Yank. That's exactly what I done.'' The tempest suddenly passed, and in its place came a cool, deadly calm.

Kit's time had run out.

''Not only rifles,'' Smythe admitted, ''but knives, traps, and even a few books published by American bookmakers.''

At the mention of books a word suddenly sprang into Kit's brain.

Heathenesse.

He had only ever heard it spoken once. Gray Feather had explained its meaning and had asked him to use it in a sentence so that he'd remember it. He'd jokingly replied, *''The wild Comanche scalped the heathenesse Ute with his butcher knife.''*

But now Kit figured he had gotten it all wrong. It wasn't the Indians who were the heathens here. It was Smythe! A man from a land that had known civilization for more than a thousand years. In that flash of revelation, Kit half regretted his words to Gray Feather.

Thinking of the Ute, he wondered if his friend was still even alive. If he should ever get out of this, and

Gray Feather had survived, Kit figured he owed his friend an—

"Marsten!" Smythe roared, suddenly taking a step back.

"Now, Gov'nor? Can I plug the Yank now?"

"Yes, you may do it now."

Grinning like a kid with his first rifle, Marsten stepped forward and put the piece to his shoulder.

Chapter Fifteen

Kit cast about for a place to leap to, but the sound of the rifle shot came almost immediately. He never had a chance to move. Instinctively, Kit winced, his eyes clamping shut. He stood there expecting to fall any second, waiting for the sharp piercing pain—a pain that never came! Was he dead already, or still alive?

The noise of horses, a sudden panicky ringing of voices, and the sound of rushing footsteps convinced him that he wasn't dead . . . at least not yet.

Kit opened his eyes and in the darkness saw men fleeing in every direction, while from the forest dark men on horseback were rushing into view. Smythe was still standing there, mouth gaping open, foot and peg seemingly riveted to the ground. A little way away Marsten lay sprawled on the dirt with his head cocked unnaturally to one side and a bloody hole in his neck spilling his life out onto the dust.

As the men scattered in different directions, the riders surrounded them and herded them back toward the firelight. It happened so fast that Kit had not yet recovered from his shock of not being dead when Chief Calling Elk rode into their midst. His warriors had every one of the Englishmen covered with their new English muskets.

"What's this all about, Calling Elk?" Smythe demanded, regaining his senses.

Calling Elk spoke to a warrior at his side. "Look over there," he said, directing the muzzle of his London Fusil at the dark, tarp-covered mound. In a moment the Indian returned carrying a well-used American Lancaster rifle similar to the one Kit owned.

"Hmm. It is as Carson said," Calling Elk grunted, narrowing his view at Smythe. "You have not spoken true words to me, Smythe. It was you all along who was doing these things, and blaming them on the Americans."

"No, that ain't true!" Smythe said.

"I heard the words from your own mouth. I heard everything."

Smythe glanced around, alarm leaping to his bearded face. Without warning he shoved Kit aside and dashed through a gap between two mounted warriors. Kit stumbled, caught himself, and dove after the fleeing Englishman. The peg leg slowed Smythe down, and he knew he'd never outrun Kit.

Smythe stopped and wheeled about, drawing his saber.

"Damn you, Carson! You surely got me killed here, but at least I'll take you to hell with me!" He lunged forward with the startling swiftness of an expert swordsman.

Kit sidestepped, arching his back just in time. The blade stabbed forward and brushed his buckskin shirt. For someone with only one leg, Smythe was amazingly fast. He recovered from the failed thrust and, using his peg as a pivot, wheeled again and slashed at Kit.

Kit ducked and felt the steel whistle across his hair. He parried a second thrust with his arm and dove for a length of firewood on the ground. Coming around, he shoved the stick up as the blade sliced a long sliver from it. Kit swung out at Smythe's leg. The club smacked into the peg, breaking it off at the cuff.

Smythe whooped in surprise, flailed his arms madly to catch his balance, then stood there wobbling on one leg. Kit was instantly up on both of his, parried Smythe's next jab, and smacked the mountain pirate in the gut. As he buckled, Kit swung and connected soundly with Smythe's skull, laying the big mountain pirate out cold on the ground.

The chief rode over and looked down at the unconscious man. Then at Kit. "He has caused much trouble for our people, and for you."

"Whal, I don't reckon he will anymore. Now he's all yours, Chief."

Kit suddenly remembered Gray Feather.

"We got to get back to your village right away, Calling Elk. Two Bulls intends to murder Gray Feather!"

Near dawn, Gray Feather groggily awoke. He was back in the village, tied to the same post he and Kit had been bound to that first day when they had been taken prisoners by Two Bulls and his warriors.

When he heard a voice at his back, he thought he must still be dreaming.

"We have no time. You must leave now," the voice was telling him. "They will be coming for you when the sun returns."

It was like a bad dream replaying itself all over again. He'd just done this, and look where it had gotten him—and where it had gotten his friend, Man With Many Horses!

But this time there was a difference. It was a woman's voice speaking softly in his ear. He felt something cold and hard slip between his wrists. The thongs parted. Gray Feather looked over his shoulder. Mary Fawn Hiding's wide eyes were staring back at him. In the faint glow of dawn he could see that they were reddened and swollen from crying.

"Man With Many Horses?" he asked, almost certain of the answer.

"My husband is dead. His one hope was that you would escape to safety. I have come to see that that desire is fulfilled."

Gray Feather almost wished she hadn't come to his rescue. He was too weak to stand, and he didn't want to be hit, punched, or shot even one more time. Dying would be a lot easier, he decided. But Mary Fawn Hiding was insistent.

"I have brought you my husband's lance. It is the only weapon I have left."

"I don't think I can stand up."

"You must. Two Bulls almost killed you earlier, but the elders stopped him. They said he must wait for our chief's return. But if Calling Elk fails to come back by morning, I know that Two Bulls will find a way to do it, in spite of what the elders wish.''

"He murdered your husband. What are the elders doing about that?''

"They do nothing.'' Her voice cracked. ''Two Bulls said that my husband turned his gun on them first. He said he only killed to defend himself.''

"That's not what happened!''

She turned her eyes to the ground, and a tear rolled off her cheek. ''It is what he said happened, and Hump and Stalking Wolf agreed with him in front of the elders.''

Gray Feather's anger gave him renewed strength. ''I must see that justice is done. Man With Many Horses did not try to kill Two Bulls.''

"Yes, I believe this. It is not how my husband would have dealt with him.''

"Help me up,'' Gray Feather demanded. She put an arm under his and together they managed to get him to his feet. ''Just get me somewhere where I can regain my strength.''

"That's not likely to happen.''

Gray Feather went rigid at the sound of Two Bulls's voice. The warrior stepped from behind one of the lodges and said in amazement, ''I did not think it possible. But now I see it before my own eyes. Two times you have been helped to escape. Hump said it would happen again, but I did not believe it possible. It is good that he convinced me to wait and watch.''

In spite of his intense pain, Gray Feather straightened up and returned the warrior's stare. ''Are you going to kill Mary Fawn Hiding now as well? And what lie will you tell to explain it to the elders this time, Two Bulls?''

"Kill her?" He gave a short laugh. "I would not think of killing my future wife."

"Never!" she spat. "I would rather cross the river of death than be joined to you."

"You will have no choice."

"My father will never give me to you!"

"Your father can be convinced," he answered confidently. The implied threat was clear in his voice. "And if he refuses, well, accidents happen. Then it will be up to your cousins to decide who you will marry. Is that not so?" he asked, glancing at the smirking Stalking Wolf.

"That is the way of our people," Stalking Wolf affirmed.

"Now, move away from him." Two Bulls motioned with the muzzle of his musket.

Mary Fawn Hiding hesitated.

"I said move!" the warrior growled.

Reluctantly, she stepped away.

Turning the musket back on Gray Feather, Two Bulls said, "Now, murderer, you will join your friend on the other side of the river of death."

"Who is the murderer here?" Gray Feather asked.

Mary Fawn Hiding took another step back, and with the attention of the three men upon Gray Feather, she slowly crouched toward the ground.

"Your double talk will not save you this time, and there is no one left to come to your—"

Two Bulls let out a sudden startled cry. His back arched forward, and at the same time the iron point of a war lance drove into it and tore out through the front of his chest. Eyes bulging, Two Bulls stared down at the crimson point that had emerged just below his left breast. Understanding came slowly to his

161

wide eyes. Turning his head, he stared helplessly at Mary Fawn Hiding standing behind him, still holding the shaft of her husband's spear in her fists.

"You?" he gasped, not believing his eyes.

"Yes. It is I who have sent you to the place where the ghosts of our people dwell. Soon you will stand before my husband, Two Bulls. You will answer to him for his murder."

Two Bulls's mouth gulped like a fish out of water, as if he wanted to say something, but no words came out, only a frothy crimson foam that bubbled thickly down his chin. The musket slipped from his fingers and Two Bulls followed it to the ground, his face frozen in wide, staring death.

Stalking Wolf and Hump stared at their leader, the shock of what had just happened momentarily numbing them. Hump came out of it first. "You've killed him!" he said, stunned. Something snapped inside his head and he turned his musket on Mary Fawn Hiding, palming back the heavy hammer.

"No!" cried Stalking Wolf. "She is my cousin."

But Hump didn't seem to hear him.

Gray Feather was in no condition to fight, but just the same he leaped. He slammed into the ground, groaning, as the pain burst in his side and shot through his body. Ignoring it, he grabbed Two Bulls's rifle and swung it around. In the dim morning light, orange flame jumped from its muzzle, and the roar that came with it had to have wakened every sleeping soul in the village.

Hump lurched backwards, his musket falling and discharging as it hit the ground.

From a dozen different lodges men clambered out bearing muskets, spears, and bows and arrows. What they saw was one dead man with a war lance thrust through his back, another with a hole torn through his chest . . . and Gray Feather still holding the rifle.

The implication was clear to everyone, and they at once fell upon Gray Feather, who was nearly dead himself. They ripped the musket from his hands and dragged him out into the center of the village, then threw him to the ground.

"He did it! He killed Hump!" Stalking Wolf shouted, urging them on.

"No, listen to me," Mary Fawn Hiding pleaded. "It is not as it appears." But no one was listening to her. There was only revenge on their minds.

Momentarily the men backed off, leaving Gray Feather to lie there staring up into their snarling faces. Then one of them came forward carrying a lance. He pressed the iron tip to Gray Feather's chest and said, "It was a mistake to let you live. Two Bulls was correct when he said we ought to have killed you and the American at once. If we had, Hump and Two Bulls would still be alive."

Gray Feather was too weak to defend himself, or even try. His wound had begun to bleed again, but he knew that the agony would soon be past. He was too weak to even plead for mercy. All he could do was lie there and watch the point suddenly lift high as the man's arm cocked back.

Gray Feather shut his eyes and waited for the final blow.

That was when the rifle shot boomed in their midst.

It brought everyone's head around. Gray Feather opened his eyes. The spear still hovered above him, but the man holding it was looking over his shoulder.

The crowd parted, and Kit Carson and Calling Elk rode into their midst, white smoke still trailing from the muzzle of Kit's rifle.

"Soaring Hawk! Do not kill him!" Calling Elk ordered.

"He killed Two Bulls and Hump," Soaring Hawk protested.

"No! My chief, it is not as he says." Mary Fawn Hiding ran up to Calling Elk's pony. "I killed Two Bulls." This brought an immediate, stunned silence. "Gray Feather killed Hump while defending me. Stalking Wolf knows the truth; make him tell you."

Calling Elk shifted his gaze to the warrior, who, under Calling Elk's withering stare, turned his eyes to the ground. The chief looked back at Mary Fawn Hiding. "I do not have to ask it. I see truth in your eyes, and only shame in his." Calling Elk raised his voice so that the whole village, which by this time had emerged from the lodges to see what was going on, could hear him. "Listen to me. We have been deceived by the man called Smythe, and by the other men with him."

As Calling Elk related all that he had learned in the last several hours, Kit slipped off the back of the horse he was riding and went to Gray Feather. No one made any move to stop him, for the chief's words had completely disarmed them. Most of the villagers were staring at Smythe and his band of trappers, each one bound to their saddles.

"You sure cut it close this time, Kit," Gray Feather said weakly.

"I figured a smart Injun like you could handle yourself." His grin faded, and he said seriously, "I'd have never left you back in that cave if I'd known this would happen.''

''Then you would have never found the truth,'' Gray Feather pointed out reasonably.

''Thar is that. They roughed you up some, I see.''

Gray Feather managed a frail laugh. ''Oh, just a little.''

Mary Fawn Hiding appeared at his side. ''Bring him to my lodge, where I can tend to his wounds.''

Kit helped Gray Feather up. To Gray Feather's surprise, two warriors who had been calling for his scalp only a few minutes before rushed over to help.

''Where is Man With Many Horses?'' Kit inquired. But he understood when he saw Gray Feather frown and Mary Fawn Hiding suddenly turn her face away. ''Sorry to hear it.''

''He died trying to help me,'' Gray Feather said.

''A lot of people have died . . .'' Kit glanced back at the big, one-eyed man astride the horse. ''. . . because of him.''

''What will the Flatheads do with him?'' Gray Feather asked.

''Don't rightly know,'' Kit admitted. ''But Calling Elk is a wise chief and a good man. Whatever he decides, I'm sure it will be the right thing.''

The sharp, crisp bite of fall was in the air when Kit and Gray Feather rode away from the Flathead village for the last time. They stopped their horses at the head of the valley to look back.

''I almost hate to leave,'' Gray Feather said, staring longingly at the scattered lodges below, each one threading a thin tendril of smoke into the clear mountain air.

"Whal, you're healed up almost like new and winter's coming on. Gotta locate Bridger and the others before the snow begins to fly. Besides, thar ain't nothing keeping us here anymore." Even as he said it, Kit knew that wasn't entirely true. Gray Feather had become enamored of Mary Fawn Hiding in the course of his recovery. Their relationship, it appeared, had grown beyond mere friendship during the month that Kit was away delivering Jim Bridger's message to Major Collins up in the Blackfoot country. Afterward Kit had traveled west to Fort Vancouver, where Calling Elk and a party of his warriors had already delivered Alexander Smythe and his men into the hands of the law.

Dr. John McLoughlin, the chief factor of the Hudson's Bay Company, had been outraged when he'd learned of Smythe's treachery. He could not believe it at first, but when Kit arrived and gave his testimony, the mountain pirate's fate had been sealed. Smythe was tried, sentenced, and executed under British law. The other members of his fur brigade were let go by the Company and ordered out of the Northwest.

All in all, Chief Calling Elk was satisfied with British justice. Kit found McLoughlin to be a fine gentleman and an attentive host. His opinion of the British climbed a few notches during his visit. But there was always a certain tension that never quite lifted until he and Calling Elk finally rode away from the fort and headed back to Flathead country.

A time was swiftly coming when the Americans and the English would have to make a treaty that each

country would abide by. Kit had learned from Mc-
Loughlin that the British had their sights set on the
Oregon territory. Unless Americans soon began to
move into it and settle that beautiful country of wide
rivers, thick trees, and rich farmland, the British
would eventually have it.

But that was something for the diplomats to dicker
over.

Kit couldn't take all the problems of the country
on his shoulders. He could, however, suggest to those
men who wanted a more settled life once their trapping days were over that Oregon might be a fair land
to check out. And that was what he was determined
to do, and to make a visit to the place sometime soon.

"Reckon you'll ever come back through this
way?" Kit inquired.

Gray Feather's frown immediately reversed itself.
"I suppose I could be talked into it, Kit."

"Will she wait for you?"

Gray Feather looked over with a start. "What are
you talking about?"

Kit laughed. "A man would have to be blind not
to see how the two of you got along."

"Kit! She hasn't yet gotten over the death of Man
With Many Horses."

"No, but she will. And when she does, I reckon
thar will be a dozen bucks wooing her all at once."
Kit winked. "You best not stay away too long, my
friend."

Gray Father didn't speak right away. When he did
he said, "What are you gonna do this winter, Kit?"

"Oh, I don't know. Figured I might go visit the
Arapaho nation for a while. Thar's a pretty little Injun
gal I met at the last rendezvous named Waa-nibe.

Thought I'd like to see her again. How about you?''

Gray Feather considered a moment. ''Maybe I'll come back this way—just to see how Mary Fawn Hiding is making out, you understand.''

''I think I understand, all right.''

Kit tried not to grin as he started his horse ahead, away from the Flathead village. But it would not be for the last time. He was almost sure of that.

KIT CARSON

The frontier adventures of a true American legend.

#2: *Ghosts of Lodore.* When Kit finds himself hurtling down the Green River into an impossibly high canyon, his first worry is to find a way out—until he comes face-to-face with a primitive Indian tribe preparing for a battle in which, one way or another, he will have to take sides.

___4325-4 $3.99 US/$4.99 CAN

#1: *The Colonel's Daughter.* Kit Carson's courage and strength as an Indian fighter have earned him respect throughout the West. And when the daughter of a Missouri colonel is kidnapped, Kit is determined to find her—even if he has to risk his life to do it!

___4295-9 $3.99 US/$4.99 CAN

DAVY CROCKETT

Sioux Slaughter. With only his long rifle and his friend, Davy Crockett sets out, determined to see the legendary splendor of the Great Plains. But it may be one gallivant too many. He barely survives a mammoth buffalo stampede before he's ambushed—by a band of Sioux warriors with blood in their eyes.

___4157-X $3.99 US/$4.99 CAN

Homecoming. The Great Lakes territories are full of Indians both peaceful and bloodthirsty. And when the brave Davy Crockett and his friend save a Chippewa maiden from warriors of a rival tribe, their travels become a deadly struggle to save their scalps.

___4112-X $3.99 US/$4.99 CAN

Dorchester Publishing Co., Inc.
P.O. Box 6640
Wayne, PA 19087-8640

Please add $1.75 for shipping and handling for the first book and $.50 for each book thereafter. NY, NYC, and PA residents, please add appropriate sales tax. No cash, stamps, or C.O.D.s. All orders shipped within 6 weeks via postal service book rate. Canadian orders require $2.00 extra postage and must be paid in U.S. dollars through a U.S. banking facility.

Name_____
Address_____
City_____State_____Zip_____
I have enclosed $_____ in payment for the checked book(s).
Payment <u>must</u> accompany all orders. ☐ Please send a free catalog.

DON'T MISS THESE OTHER GREAT STORIES IN

 **The Lost Wilderness Tales**

DODGE TYLER

In the days of the musket, the powder horn, and the flintlock, one pioneer ventures forth into the virgin land that will become the United States.

#5: Apache Revenge. A band of Apaches with blood in their eyes ride the warpath right to Dan'l's door, looking to avenge their humiliating defeat at his hands three years earlier. And when they capture Dan'l's niece as a trophy it becomes more than just a battle for Dan'l, it becomes personal. No matter where the warriors ride, the frontiersman swears to find them, to get the girl back—and to exact some vengeance of his own.

_4183-9   **$4.99 US/$5.99 CAN**

#4: Winter Kill. Gold fever—the treacherous disease caused the vicious ends of many pioneers. One winter, Dan'l finds himself making a dangerous trek for lost riches buried in lands held sacred by the Sioux. Soon, Boone is fighting with all his skill and cunning to win a battle against hostile Sioux warriors, ferocious animals, and a blizzard that would bury a lesser man in a horrifying avalanche of death.

_4087-5   **$4.99 US/$5.99 CAN**

Dorchester Publishing Co., Inc.
P.O. Box 6640
Wayne, PA 19087-8640

Please add $1.75 for shipping and handling for the first book and $.50 for each book thereafter. NY, NYC, and PA residents, please add appropriate sales tax. No cash, stamps, or C.O.D.s. All orders shipped within 6 weeks via postal service book rate. Canadian orders require $2.00 extra postage and must be paid in U.S. dollars through a U.S. banking facility.

Name_____
Address_____
City_____State_____Zip_____
I have enclosed $_____ in payment for the checked book(s).
Payment <u>must</u> accompany all orders. ❏ Please send a free catalog.

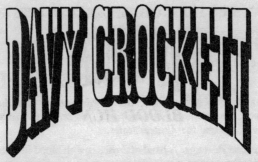

HOMECOMING

DAVID THOMPSON

Davy Crockett lives for adventure. With a faithful friend at his side and a trusty long rifle in his hand, the fearless frontiersman sets out for the Great Lakes territories. But the region surrounding the majestic inland seas is full of Indians both peaceful and bloodthirsty. And when the brave pioneer saves a Chippewa maiden from warriors of a rival tribe, his travels become a deadly struggle to save his scalp. If Crockett can't defeat his fierce foes, the only remains he'll leave will be his legend and his coonskin cap.

___4112-X $3.99 US/$4.99 CAN

Dorchester Publishing Co., Inc.
P.O. Box 6640
Wayne, PA 19087-8640

Please add $1.75 for shipping and handling for the first book and $.50 for each book thereafter. NY, NYC, and PA residents, please add appropriate sales tax. No cash, stamps, or C.O.D.s. All orders shipped within 6 weeks via postal service book rate. Canadian orders require $2.00 extra postage and must be paid in U.S. dollars through a U.S. banking facility.

Name_____
Address_____
City_____State_____Zip_____
I have enclosed $_____ in payment for the checked book(s).
Payment <u>must</u> accompany all orders. ❏ Please send a free catalog.

BLOOD HUNT

David Thompson

With only his oldest friend and his trusty long rifle for company, Davy Crockett explores the wild frontier looking for adventure, and has the strength and cunning to face any enemy. But even he may have met his match when he gets caught between two warring tribes on one side and a dangerous band of white men on the other—all of them willing to die—and kill—for a group of stolen women. It is up to Crockett to save the women, his friend and his own hide if he wants to live to explore another day.

_4229-0 $3.99 US/$4.99 CAN

Dorchester Publishing Co., Inc.
P.O. Box 6640
Wayne, PA 19087-8640

CHEYENNE

DOUBLE EDITION
JUDD COLE

One man's heroic search for a world he can call his own.

Arrow Keeper. A Cheyenne raised among pioneers, Matthew Hanchon has never known anything but distrust. The settlers brand him a savage, and when Matthew realizes that his adopted parents will suffer for his sake, he flees into the wilderness—where he'll need a warrior's courage if he hopes to survive.

And in the same volume...

Death Chant. When Matthew returns to the Cheyenne, he doesn't find the acceptance he seeks. The Cheyenne can't fully trust any who were raised in the ways of the white man. Forced to prove his loyalty, Matthew faces the greatest challenge he has ever known.

___4280-0 $4.99 US/$5.99 CAN